H. Parker Fitch

The Pathway of Fire

H. Parker Fitch

The Pathway of Fire

ISBN/EAN: 9783337255541

Printed in Europe, USA, Canada, Australia, Japan

Cover: Foto ©Andreas Hilbeck / pixelio.de

More available books at **www.hansebooks.com**

THE

PATHWAY OF FIRE,

OR

Baptist Principles Traced By the Efforts to Exterminate Them.

By H. P. FITCH.

Author of "Through Shadow to Sunshine." "Saved By
His Wife," "At the Temple Gate," Etc.

"I will leave in the midst of thee an afflicted and
poor people, and they shall trust in the name of the
Lord."

REV. H. P. FITCH.

CONTENTS.

To the

memory of

Rev. R. A. Fyfe, D. D.

At whose feet I first learned

to love the study of that "Pathway of Fire,"

so long trodden by the feet of our

fathers, this little volume is af-

fectionately dedicated by

the author.

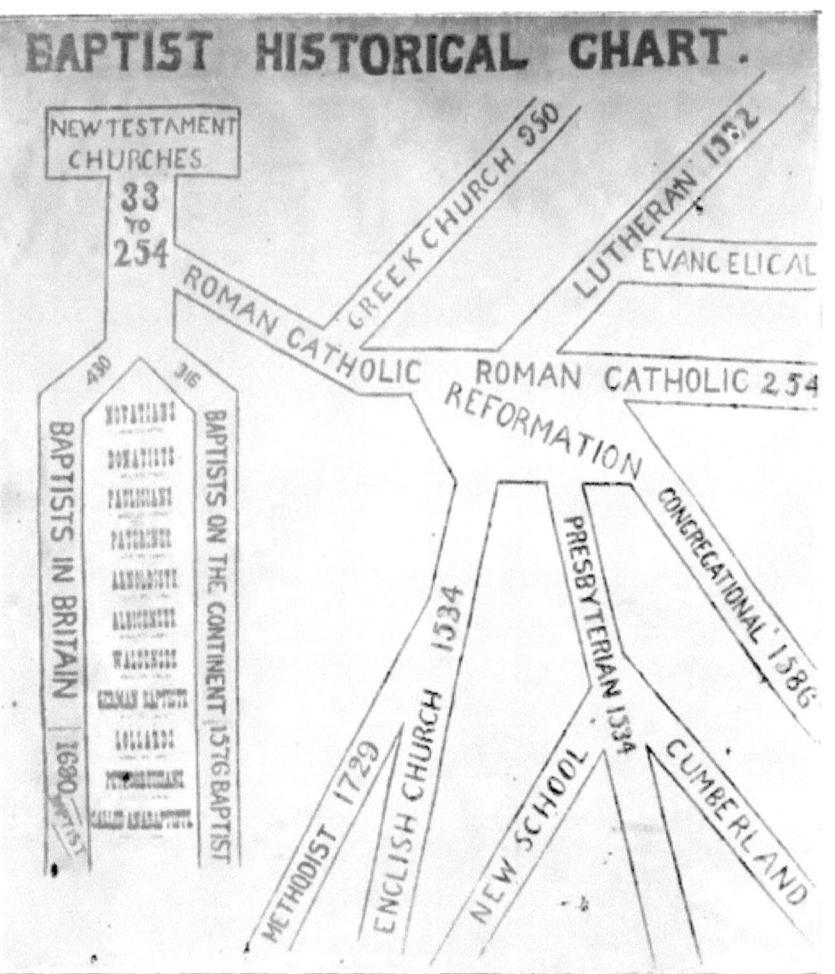

THE PATHWAY OF FIRE.

The Pathway of Fire.

PRELIMINARY CHAPTER.

Most of the writers who have written on the subject of Baptist History, have gone to one or the other of two extremes. One class are those who insist on the necessity and possibility of tracing an unbroken succession of Baptist churches, from the days of the Apostles; one church, through its regularly constituted administrator, transmitting its apostolic baptism to another church following it.

This is as unnecessary as it is impossible. It is never wise for any religious denomination to claim more than they can substantiate; and this is especially unwise, when such claims are entirely unnecessary. Wherever possible, baptism should be administered by a regularly constituted administrator, as it tends, the better, to preserve the "order of the Lord's house;" but genuine apostolic succession consists in "keeping the ordinances as they were delivered" rather than in the simple act of transmitting baptism from one to another. Wherever you find an assembly of converted men and women, who, as such, have been immersed on the profession of their faith in Christ, as a personal Savior, and have united themselves together in the fellowship of the Gospel, to maintain the worship and ordinances of Christ, there you have true apostolic succession.

Had this truth always been kept in mind, it would have spared much useless labor, in efforts to substantiate what neither Scripture nor reason requires.

The class who go to the other extreme, are those who deny the possibility of tracing an unbroken line of Baptist principles from the days of the apostles until now. This is equally a mistake with the other. A succession of Baptist churches we do not claim because it is not necessary; a succession of Baptist principles we do claim, and that claim can be made good. From the days of Christ until now, there has never been a period in which we cannot trace a people, holding the principles and doctrines, and following the practices that essentially characterize the Baptists of the present day.

The author of this little book wishes it understood, therefore, that it is not his intention to write a history of the Baptist denomination. He believes the middle ground between the two extremes, above mentioned, to be the correct one. He firmly believes that there can be traced an unbroken chain of Baptist principles, down through the ages, from the first to the nineteenth century. He will not attempt to cover all the ground, even, in this field of study. That would make the book too large for his purpose. He wishes it for the masses, and will condense the matter as much as is consistent with a clear narrative.

One or two further facts should also be stated, however, before proceeding with our narrative. One is that not all of those who protested against the corruptions of the Roman Catholics, the Greek church, or other state churches through all those ages, were Baptists. Here, I think, is where some writers of Baptist history have made a mistake. For instance, they have claimed that all who went by the name of "Anabaptists," were, in both principles and practice, our own people. This has not only rendered them subject to criticism, but has furnished those who essentially differ from the Baptists with strong arguments against their claim to antiquity. They have been able to prove that some, at least, of those who have been claimed as Baptists, were, in some of their practices, quite different from our people of modern times, and they have argued that if some of those whom the Baptists claim are proven to be otherwise than genuine Baptists, it is reasonable to conclude that they were all alike different, and the claim to Baptist antiquity therefore falls to the ground.

The truth is that there can be found, as we pass down the ages, people in all stages of separation, from the great hierarchies that have stood out so prominently on the pages of history, for their power and persecuting spirit. Even the term "Anabaptist" does not, in all cases, indicate a people, in doctrine and prac-

tice, in all particulars, similar to our own. For
instance, after the apostolic practice of believers' immersion had, to a great extent, been
superseded by the immersion of infants, and
later, by the sprinkling of infants. there were
some so-called Anabaptists who, while they refused to recognize any but believers as scriptural subjects of baptism, were content to adopt
the new custon of sprinkling and pouring.
This, of course, refers only to the period from
the beginning of the fifteenth to about the middle of the sixteenth centuries. Up to the former period, immersion was the almost universal
custom, and. therefore, wherever we find believers' baptism, we find believers' immersion.
After that date, for at least a hundred and fifty
years, we need to be very careful lest we claim
as Baptists, many who materially differed
from us, in one of the essential characteristics
of a Baptist church, namely, the act of immersion as positively essential to New Testament'
baptism. Baptists there were, and they adhered tenaciously to this New Testament practice, while many others of the same name, accepted, and followed the teachings of men,
rather than the commandments of Christ.
While this was partly, no doubt, from choice,
there can be no question, in many instances,
that it was the result of the hand of persecution laid so heavily upon them, compelling
them to hide their principles, and worship God
in secret.

Another fact to be borne in mind is, that, as

we may readily understand, all those people of whom we write, were influenced, more or less, by the manners and customs of the people and age in which they lived. It would be unreasonable for us to expect to find in the early centuries the refinement of civilization, as we understand it, we have in the present age. The fact that they were influenced by the manners and customs, the learning and philosophy of their age, does not, in the least, prove them to be unbaptistic or any the less New Testament Christians. This is an important consideration, and should not be lost sight of as we follow their pathway through the ages. In writing this I am not forgetful of the fact that the pen of persecution has attacked their memory, even as the sword of persecution attacked their person. It is, however, enough for us to know that he who has provided a place for their "souls under the altar," and furnished them with "white robes, bidding them to be patient," will, in his own good time, reveal to men, as he has already revealed to angels, the grandeur of their principles and the heroism of their lives.

With this brief preliminary statement, let us away to our task of tracing the footsteps of our fathers along their fiery pathway through the ages.

CHAPTER I.

FINDING THE PATH.

"Ask for the old paths; where is the good way?"

To one who delights in the truth, and loves to follow its footsteps, there can be no more interesting and profitable study, than to trace the history of pure christianity, in its devious windings down through the ages of the past. To follow it, as starting from its Divine fountain head, it flows, like a clear pellucid stream, now through some rugged mountain defile, where the great towering rocks frown down upon him—now through some dark forest glen, where the thorns and briars of the world's petty hatred scratch and annoy him—then through some pleasant meadow vale, where on either side, stretch the green fields and fragrant flowers of religious thought and freedom—now almost lost to sight beneath the overhanging arches and matted brambles of superstition and error; until, at last, it flows out in the clear, broad unruffled stream of pure gospel truth—ever growing deeper and broader, as its crystal waters flow onward, distributing their life-giving influences to the nations of the earth. Such, in a word, is the history of Baptist principles, from the days of the apostles, until now.

And yet, let me assure the reader, there are but few studies that he will pursue with more mingled feelings of pleasure and pain; or in which he will need to exercise greater caution, if he would arrive at the exact truth. Not because God has failed to keep alive the lamp of Divine Christianity, during all these days of the church's tribulation, "when the Man of Sin sat upon his seven hills, and from his throne of darkness ruled the world." Not because Christ's altar-fires were left to languish and expire, and leave the world in darkness. Ah no! for as God, in the days of Elijah, had reserved to himself seven thousand men, who had never bowed the knee to Baal or to his image, so, never since the gospel light first shone o'er Judea's plains, has he allowed it to become extinguished.

There are several things, however, that combine to render the study an exceedingly difficult one. In the first place special care is necessary to separate the true from the false; and to distinguish between that which, like pure gold will stand the test of the hot fires of persecution, and the dross, which the fire only consumes, and which fails to measure up to the infallible Bible standard.

Then, again, the careless student is in great danger of being caught by the glare and glitter, the pomp and pageantry, and gorgeous ritualism of corrupt state organizations. Here is where so many of our so-called church histories fail. They are almost exclusively histories of *churchianity*, instead of *christianity*. There is ample history of the former, that is, of the great religious hierarchy, the church of Rome— indeed, of all those proud haughty state organizations, but if we would look for the foot-prints of pure gospel christianity, we must follow some humbler and more obscure path than that taken by those churches that joined in an unholy alliance with worldly state power.

Still another thing that combines to make this a difficult study, is the scarcity of reliable data from which to arrive at the exact truth. It must be borne in mind, as Dean Waddington so tersely puts it, that all the information we get of those early religious bodies, whom we, as Baptists, are wont to regard as our fathers in tribulation, is derived from their enemies. It will not do to put too much reliance on the testimony of a witness, when we know the witness is an implacable enemy. I am sorry to see that even some Baptist writers have fallen somewhat into this error. When we remember that for centuries it was the policy of Rome to misrepresent, to persecute, to deny every civil and religious right, and to falsely brand as heretics—to destroy and kill by sword and stake, and faggot and fire, those despised followers of Jesus, whose only crime was allegiance to Christ and his word, the wonder is that there is left to us of the nineteenth century, any testimony whatever of the Scripturalness of their doctrines or the purity of their lives. Their books were burned, their records destroyed, their members butchered and their property confiscated.

And yet, in spite of all, God has himself kept the records, and in these last days he is gathering them up, and with trumpet tongue, they are witnessing to the grandeur of that heroism and devotion to truth which prompted those martyred saints to choose death in its most horrid forms rather than to surrender their fidelity to Christ, or worship at the shrine of a corrupt state church. From the musty, mouldering piles of their old court records, from the long hidden decrees of kings and councils, and vaticans, from the bitter curses and anathemas hurled like bolts of thunder at those true worshipers.

"Who kept the truth so pure of old,"

from the admissions and contradictions of their enemies—from all these God is bringing out and flinging to the world the truth concerning those ancient martyrs of Jesus. "It is the Lord's doings and marvellous in our eyes."

Let us assure the reader that it is through no pleasant, flowery vale that much of his pathway will lie as he traces the footprints of pure christianity down through those twelve hundred and sixty years, in which her true followers witnessed in sack-cloth, and held aloft the lamp of divine truth, amid the dense spiritual darkness, that the world might know that Christ still had a church upon the earth. He

will trace it by the cruel edicts that were passed
for its extermination. He will follow it by the
light of the fires that were kindled to consume
its faithful witnesses who could die but could
not prove false to the faith they had received.
He will trace it by the groans and cries that
come from darkened prisons and loathsome
dungeons where the victims of the inquisition
languished and prayed and died and are forgotten. By the blood-dyed streams of Europe—
by the flashing signal fire where it gleams from
some rocky height to warn the fleeing, persecuted fugitive where he might find an asylum
and a hiding place from the fury of his murder-
ers. From Africa's sands and Armenia's
snows—from Alpine summits and Piedmont's
vales—from the scattered ashes where Smithfield's fires formed a chariot in which God's
redeemed ones rode to glory and to God—by the
voices that come to him from the "souls that
were under the altar" as thy cry "How long
oh Lord?"—yea, by all these he can trace that
"Pathway of Fire" so long trodden by our fathers that we, their descendents, with the rest
of mankind, may enjoy the blessing of an open
Bible and a pure christianity.

CHAPTER II.

CORRECTING MISTAKES.

" He will teach us His ways and we will walk in His paths."

Before beginning our search for "the true origin of that sect," now known as Baptists, I desire to pause and correct one or two errors in regard thereto, which, without so intending, doubtless, by those who propagate them, nevertheless do our Baptist people an injustice. I refer first to the determined effort made by so many modern writers and speakers to show that American Baptists owe their origin to and descent from Roger Williams; and second, that other statement that "the Baptist denomination are sprung from the 'Mad Men of Munster'," that city in Westphalia where, in 1534, occurred a semi-political, semi-religious uprising of the people who attempted to establish an ideal government of their own; and led on by ambitious and fanatical leaders, committed excesses from which the Baptists of their times would have turned away with loathing.

Concerning the first mistake—that which makes the American Baptists descend from Roger Williams—it is not my intention to enter into the controversy that has grown out of the very strange statement of Rev. Dr. Whitsitt, in Johnson's Cyclopedia, to the effect that the

"baptism of Roger Williams was most likely by
sprinkling." How it was possible, with all the
facts and evidences existing, for Dr. Whitsitt,
to make such a statement I am at a loss to deter-
mine, for if any historical fact has been clearly
and satisfactorily settled, it is that in 1639, at
the newly planted colony at what is now the
city of Providence, Rhode Island, Roger Williams, Ezekiel Hollman and a number of others
decided to organize themselves into a Baptist
church. That they appointed Hollman to immerse Williams, who in turn immersed Hollman and the rest and thus completed their organization.

For this baptism of Williams and his associates, the Baptists have no apology to make.
New Testament baptism derives its authority,
not from history, but from the New Testament.
Under the circumstances, that band of believers
was Scripturally justified in refusing anything
but New Testament baptism, in act, with the
best possible administrator at hand. When, as
an assembly of believers, acting on their belief,
in New Testament teachings, they appointed
one of their number to carry out Christ's commandment, they came under the Divine rule
laid down in Second Corinthians, 8:12.

All this, however, in justice to that church,
and as a Scriptural truth. So far from the
church thus organized by Roger Williams,
being the parent of American Baptist churches,
it has not, and never had, any place in American
Baptist history, as I will presently show.

Baptists do not honor Roger Williams as their founder in America, but as the first man to plant on American soil, the flag of soul liberty. As a matter of fact, there was no genuine liberty of conscience in America, till Roger Williams learned it, loved it, and suffered for it. Unfortunately that pernicious error—the right of the State to control in matters of religion, after kindling the fires of Smithfield, and covering Europe with the graves of martyred dead, embarked with the Puritans in the Mayflower, and landed on the shores of the new world.

Roger Williams was the first man in America possessing the courage, the heroic faith, to put his foot on the head of the monster, and crush out its life. For this act, not because he is the "Father of American Baptists," he is justly entitled to be honorably remembered, not only by every Baptist, but every American citizen who cherishes freedom or loves soul liberty.

Here, also, comes in the Scriptural beauty of Baptist church independence. Had that church remained, it would have simply formed one of the many thousands of Baptist churches with which America has been covered. It might even have contended for the honor of being the oldest Baptist church in America, but that is all. Each church in all the great Baptist family derives its authority to exist from the living Word, and not from any other Baptist church. All this, however, has nothing to do with American Baptist history. As a historical fact, the church formed by Williams and his associates continued only during the space of four months. From some cause Williams withdrew and allowed the church to become scattered and the members to seek a home as opportunity offered, elsewhere. We have no doubt whatever that there was an overruling Providence in this, so directing, that while the hero of soul-liberty should plant deep in the soil of the New World that God-given principle of freedom for which Baptists have contended for nineteen centuries, so far as their history is concerned, the position of American Baptists might remain forever unassailable.

At the proper place in this narrative I will give the facts, touching the early history of the Baptists of this country; at present this is all that is necessary to say on the subject.

The other error is that which refers the origin of the Baptists to the "Mad Men of Munster." On this point, to those who are willing to accept a plain, truthful statement of facts, proven beyond a shadow of doubt by facts and dates that are indisputable, it is unnecessary to dwell at great length. I can understand how this mistake came to be, at first made, and have no harsh words to write of those, who, by their constant reiteration of this statement, as to their origin, have done the Baptists this great injustice. I presume the mistake grew out of the similarity of the names, Munzer and Munster. Though these names are of familiar sound, there is no more relation between them, than there is between the light of the Sun at noonday and that of a flaming torch at midnight. Munzer is the name of that heroic Baptist martyr, who died at the hand of his persecutors in 1525, by being cruelly beheaded. Munster was the city in Westphalia where the revolt, known as that of the "Mad Men of Munster," occurred in 1534, nine years after Thomas Munzer had heroically sealed his allegiance to Christ with his blood and had gone up along "The fiery pathway" to wear the martyr's crown and rest forever with angels and with God.

It is true that those men of Munster committed excesses, and indulged in practices—albeit they practiced immersion, even, as the Baptists have always done—for which no Baptist will apologize; but it must not be forgotten that they were men who had been driven to desperation by the conduct of their oppressors. Crushed beneath the iron heel of a despotism, as relentless and cruel as the world has ever known, it is scarcely to be wondered that those ignorant peasants would mistake lawlessness for liberty.

The facts concerning that outbreak are, that the Baptists had nothing, whatever, to do with it; nor was there any act, save that they immersed those who joined them, that could afford the slightest ground for styling them Baptists, or even Anabaptists. Their principal leader was a Lutheran named Rothman; and it is as unjust to refer the crimes and indecencies of Rothman and his followers to the Baptists of those days as it would be to blame the handful of peaceable Baptists now seeking to do their Master's work in Cuba, for all the horrors and calamities that are now rending that unhappy island. Nor have I the least doubt but that if there were no source of information concerning the heroic efforts which those Cuban patriots are making for their freedom from the galling yoke of Spanish tyranny, save that which we would get through Spanish representation, they would appear in a scarcely more favorable light, than do those "Mad Men" who fought and bled and died at Munster. And who knows but that, when in the time to come, the search-light of truth, pure and simple, may be turned on that Munster affair, those same mad men may present as much the appearance of heroes as they do now of demons.

No, kind reader. If you would find "the true origin of that sect called the Baptists" you must go back beyond the days of Roger Williams, though we honor him for his devotion to soul liberty; back beyond the "Mad Men of Munster," though I doubt if even they were as black as their enemies have painted them; back beyond the days of Luther and Calvin and Knox, though the world should do honor to their name and memory for the noble stand they took and the mighty blows they struck in favor of an open Bible and a purer church; back beyond the blood-dyed valleys of Piedmont and Wales, back beyond the millions who died a martyr's death and in chariots of literal fire went up to Glory

and to God—back beyond the decrees of kings,
the bulls of Popes, the decisions of councils,
and the thunderings of the Vatican—back,
back along the pathway lighted by the altar
fires of consecrated allegiance to Christ and his
truth, as well as the glaring red torch from the
martyr fires of persecution, nor stop till you
reach that little upper room in the far away city
of Jerusalem nineteen centuries ago, if you
would find the origin of that body of christians,
now known to the whole world as the Baptist
denomination.

I cannot more appropriately close this chapter than by quoting the testimony of that prince
of church historians, Dr. Mosheim, himself a
Lutheran and professor of church history in
the University of Gottingen, Germany.

He says: "The true origin of that sect
that derived the name Anabaptist from their
administering anew the rite of baptism to such
as came to them from the Roman Catholic
church, is hidden in the remotest depths of antiquity; and is therefore, very difficult to deter-
mine. Before the rise of Luther and Calvin,
there lay concealed in nearly all the countries
of Europe, particularly in Bohemia, Moravia,
Switzerland and Germany an innumerable company of persons who adhered tenaciously to the
doctrines of the Dutch Baptists. They believed
that the kingdom of Christ, or visible church
which he established on the earth was an assembly of the true and real saints; and ought,
therefore, to be inaccessible to the wicked and

unrighteous and also exempt from all those institutions which human prudence suggests to oppose the progress of iniquity or to correct and reform transgressors. McLean's, P. 490.

For this frank and truthful testimony of Mosheim to the ancient origin of the Baptists, he is entitled to the thanks of all lovers of truthful representation. At the same time we may find "the true origin of the Baptists" if we look for it in the right direction. To a study of that origin, I now invite the attention of the reader.

CHAPTER III.

THE PLACE OF STARTING.

"Out of Zion shall go forth the law and the Word of the Lord from Jerusalem."

"Repentance and remission of sins shall be preached in my name, beginning at Jerusalem."

In these two Scriptures we have clearly a prophesy and its fulfillment. The divine plan and purpose regarding the work of salvation is here unfolded. Seven hundred years before the angel's song announced to the Shepherds of Galilee the advent of the Son of God, Isaiah foretold that Jerusalem should be the place whence should go forth the Divine proclamation of Salvation. In the fullness of time, this prophesy was fulfilled. Christ came, and by his vicarious death made possible the Salvation of all the people. Then, as showing the oneness of the Divine purpose in the fulfillment of prophesy, he commanded his disciples to "Go into all the world and preach the gospel to every creature, beginning at Jerusalem."

In the furtherence of this Divine purpose, and as a human means for carrying it out, Christ organized what he termed the church. To that church he gave certain doctrines, ordinances and commands with positive instructions that they were to be retained, practiced and obeyed, even until the end of time. Fur-

ther, that these doctrines and duties might be
fully known and understood, he chose twelve
men whom he kept under his direct teaching
for three and a half years. And further still,
that they might be rendered incapable of mistake, he commanded them to tarry at Jerusalem
till they should be endued with wisdom from on
high. For ten days they did nothing but pray
and wait for this Divine enduement. At the
end of that time the Holy Spirit came down
upon them in such wondrous power that they
became completely under his Divine influence
and control.

Why was all this? The answer is plain. It
was necessary to render them incapable of mistake. In their methods, their teachings, their
organizations, their doctrines and practices
those disciples were to stand as models for all
coming time. What they were to preach was
to form the theme of Gospel preaching, so long
as the world should stand. The plans and
methods which they should adopt, were to be
the plans and methods of the church so long as
time should last. In the material of which
their churches were composed, in the ordinances Christ had given, and the doctrines they
should teach their churches, until the end of the
dispensation were to constitute the Divinely
given models by which all church work should
be done.

I desire to emphasize this important truth.
It is too often overlooked and the idea allowed
to prevail that certain latitude was given to the

church to change what Christ and his apostles commanded and practiced. This is a grievous error. Never, till "the end of the world" was the church to depart one iota from the plain instructions given by Christ, or the doctrines and ordinances taught and practiced by the Apostles. In every respect, their churches were to represent the churches of Christ, until he should "come the second time, without sin unto Salvation."

From that Divinely constructed model nothing was to be taken, to it nothing was to be added.

All that is necessary, therefore, for us is to study those Divinely given models and "to make all things according to the pattern." And if we wish to know how far our work today is correct or incorrect, we have only to compare it with the Divine model, and the matter is at once settled.

Before we start on our journey into "the remotest depths of antiquity" in search of "the true origin of that sect, called the Baptists," let us take a photograph of the Baptist churches of today, that we may the more easily identify those of our brethren wherever we shall meet them in the ages of long ago. In other words, let us study briefly the characteristics of the Baptist churches of to-day, in their doctrines and ordinances, compare them with those of the Apostolic churches and then see if we can trace the same characteristic principles and practices, down through the intervening ages.

First—The Baptist churches are composed only of those who have repented of their sins, confessed Christ as a personal Savior and been immersed on the profession of their faith.

Second.—The Baptists are in no sense a hierarchy. Each church is an independent local assembly of baptised believers. It is independent of all other churches, democratic in its form of government, acknowledging no head but Christ, and no law but his word.*

Third.—The Baptists accept nothing but the Bible as the only rule of faith and practice, and the sole arbiter in matters of religion.

Fourth.—The Baptists practice as ordinances only the two positive commands of Christ; baptism and the Lord's supper. The former consists of the immersion of a believer in water, in the name of the Trinity; the latter in partaking of simple bread and wine in token of the broken body and shed blood of the Lord Jesus Christ.

To these may be added the fact that the Baptists do not trace their history to, nor have they, in any way, been connected with the church of Rome. They are not Protestants, in the sense of having come out of, or dating their origin from the Roman Catholic church. I have nothing but words of commendation for those illustrious men who dared to defy the power of Rome and contend for an open Bible and a purer

---

*It is an historical fact of which the Baptists may well be proud, that the Constitution of the United States, was framed after the model, found in a local Baptist church in the State of Virginia.

church. Let the names of Luther and Calvin and Knox and Foster and Brown and Wesley and a host of others be enshrined in the most sacred archives of their church's history. It was not their fault that they were born and reared within the influence of a corrupt state church. Not their fault that their spiritual mother became so corrupt that they could no longer repose under the old roof-tree where they had been born and where they had been reared. But it is to their great honor on earth and will be to their glory in Heaven that they had the moral courage to break the chain with which they were bound, and step out into the clearer light of the gospel and to grasp the grand truth of Salvation by faith.

But in this narrative I am dealing, not with sentiment, but with historical fact. If, then, God has been pleased to give the Baptists a still grander heritage, to him be all the glory. And that grander heritage he has given us. If it be honorable in the sight of God and men to protest against the corruption of a proud, persecuting, religious hierarchy, then, indeed may the Baptists claim the greater honor; for certain it is they have protested longer and protested louder than any of their brethren—yea, protested, even to the death, for spiritual religion and a gospel church. The difference, however, is this. Their protests have all been made outside of the church of Rome. Running parallel with her down the ages, there has been no age in which Rome has not met a protesting spirit in those witnesses for the truth which the Baptists of to-day claim as their fathers.

How far and in what respect do the churches of the New Testament compare in doctrine and practice with the Baptist churches of today? A careful examination will reveal the fact that, in all essential characteristics, the Apostolic churches were precisely the same as our modern Baptist churches.

First.—It is evident that among the Apostolic churches none were received into fellowship, except such as had professed faith in Christ as a personal Savior and gave evidence of genuine repentance from sin. This is so plain that it seems unnecessary to discuss it. On the day of Penticost when the Holy Spirit had convicted the multitude of sin, and they asked what they should do, Peter struck the keynote of the Gospel. "Repent and be baptised every one of you." "Then they that gladly received the word were baptised." When "Philip went down to the City of Samaria and preached Christ unto them," we are told that "When they believed Philip's preaching * * * * they were baptised, both men and women." When the Ethiopian Eunich asked baptism at the hands of this same evangelist, the answer was: "If thou believest with all thy heart, thou mayest."

The same rule was observed all through the apostolic age. Wherever they preached, wherever they organized a church, the theme of their preaching was repentance from sin and faith in Christ; to be followed immediately by immersion and membership in the church. In support of this, the reader is referred to the testimony of Neander, Mosheim, and all other church historians, who have written of that early age. All testify to the fact, so plainly self-evident, that the apostolic churches were composed only of those who had been baptised on the profession of their faith.

Nor is it less plain that, in the second characteristic, the New Testament churches were similar to modern Baptist churches. Each church was an independent, local assembly of baptised believers.

It has become customary to speak of each religious denomination as a church. As for instance, the Baptist church, the Methodist church, etc. While this is allowable, it must be remembered that it is only the modern, not the New Testament signification of the term; and it was not so used or understood in the apostolic churches.

Those churches were the farthest possible removed from anything like a religious hierarchy. Each church was independent of all other churches. Hence, when the inspired writer would speak of the whole body of christians, he would use the plural form, "churches;" as for instance, "Hear what the Spirit saith unto the churches," "The seven churches of Asia," "Then had the churches rest, and, walking in the fear of the Lord, were edified."

When writing to or of the brethren in a certain locality, the singular is used, as the church at Corinth, the church at Philippi, the church at Rome, the church at Ephesus—just as the Baptists of to-day have the church at Cleveland, the church at Knoxville; the local church of any other single locality—or the Baptist churches of Tennessee or of the United States. As the historian, Dean Waddington, so tersely puts it, "Every church was essentially independent of every other." They acknowledged no head but Christ, and no law but his word.

Third.—Allegiance to Christ and his law, was another grand characteristic of the New Testament, as it is, and has been of the Baptist churches. When Peter uttered that brief compendium of New Testament church faith, "Whether it be right to obey God, rather than man, judge ye, for we cannot but speak the things that we have heard and seen," he laid down the fundamental principal of law, by which the true churches of Jesus Christ have been governed in all ages, from the first church at Jerusalem, till the present day.

Fourth.—In their officers the New Testament churches were also similar to our modern Baptists. Their officers were simply Pastors, or bishops and deacons. A single reference to Acts 20th will show that the office of elder and that of bishop were one and the same. We read there that "Paul sent to Ephesus and called the elders of the church." When they arrived he addressed them as "overseers." These words in the original are the same words we have translated elders and bishops. Mosheim, in his church history, is very careful to warn us against confounding the bishops of the present day with the simple pastors of the churches in the apostolic days. The former, he says, was only the pastor of a single church in which he acted more the part of a servant than that of the master.

Fifth.—In their ordinances the churches of the New Testament were precisely similar to our modern Baptist churches. They were the same in their subjects. They were such as professed faith in Christ. They were the same in the act of baptism. It was the immersion of a believer in water. They were the same in their observance of the Lord's supper. This was, to quote Mosheim, "The communion of the faithful." Simply partaking of bread and wine, in commemoration of Christ.

Nothing could be more simple than the observance of Christ's ordinances by the New Testament churches. In the simplest manner possible, they carried out their dear Lord's commission to "Go teach all nations, baptising them in the name of the Father, Son and Holy Spirit, teaching them to observe all things, whatsoever I have comanded you."

As this is the point around which centers the greatest controversy, I will pause here to introduce a chapter of testimony, in proof of the positions I have taken, as to the characteristics of the New Testament churches.

CHAPTER IV.

A CHAPTER OF TESTIMONY.

"Ye are my witnesses saith the Lord."

In the last chapter we considered the various characteristics of the New Testament churches and their perfect resemblance to those of modern Baptists. In this chapter we shall present a mass of testimony in proof of our position as to those characteristics.

These points of resemblance refer to their membership, their church polity and government, their allegiance to Christ and his word, their officers and their ordinances. Without taking the trouble to group each separate testimony under its respective head, I will present the whole mass of evidence that the reader can see how strongly our position is fortified. This testimony, to any fair minded reader, cannot fail to be convincing. Indeed, to anyone honestly, and carefully examining the New Testament, this testimony will be superflous; but as many people look for human testimony to affirm Divine records, I give it. The authorities can be consulted by the reader if he so desires.

Let us first introduce the testimony of Church historians on these points of similarity between the present Baptist and apostolic churches.

Neander, on the subject of baptism says: "Baptism was administered, at first, only to adults as men were accustomed to conceive baptism and faith as strictly connected." As to the mode, he says, "Baptism was originally administered by immersion; and many of the comparisons of St. Paul allude to this form of administration. Immersion is a symbol of being buried with Christ and coming forth from the water, a symbol of resurrection with Christ."

Bishop Taylor:—"There is no pretense of tradition that the church in all ages baptised infants."

Salmacius Suicerus:—"In the first two centuries no one was baptised except being instructed in the faith and acquainted with the doctrines of Christ, he was able to profess himself a believer."

M. De. La. Roque:—"The primitive church did not baptise infants."

Mosheim. First century—"The sacrament of baptism was administered in this century without the public assembly, in places appointed and prepared for the purpose and was performed by the immersion of the whole body in the baptismal font."

Second century.—"The sacrament of baptism was administered publicly twice a year, at Easter and Whitsuntide. The persons that were to be baptised, after they had repeated the creed, confessed and renounced their sins, and particularly the devil and his pompous allurements were immersed under water and received into Christ's Kingdom by a solemn invocation of Father, Son and Holy Ghost, according to the express command of our blessed Lord."

Dean Waddington.—"The ceremony of immersion, the oldest form of baptism, was performed in the name of the three persons of the Trinity."

Cave.—"The party to be baptised was wholly immerged or put under water, which was the almost constant and universal custom of those times."

Bishop Taylor.—"The custom of the ancient church was not sprinkling but immersion; in pursuance of the sense of the word (baptise) and the commandment and example of our blessed Savior."

Bossuet.—"We read not in the Scriptures that baptism was otherwise (than by immersion) administered; and we are able to make it appear by the acts of councils, and by the ancient rituals, that, for thirteen hundred years, baptism was thus administered, throughout the whole church as far as possible."

Dr. Wall.—"Their (the primitive christian's) general and ordinary way was to baptise by immersion. This is so plain and clear, by an infinite number of passages, that as we cannot but pity the weak endeavors of such Pedobaptists, as would maintain the negative of it, so also we ought to disown and show a dislike for the profane scoffs of the English Antipedobaptists, merely for their use of dipping. It was in all probability, the way in which our blessed

Savior, and for certain was the most usual and ordinary way by which the ancient christians did receive their baptism. As for sprinkling, I say, as Mr. Blake, at its first coming up in England, let them defend it who use it."

Dr. Philip Schaff.—As to the mode of baptism says: "It is unquestionably the fact, that the mode of baptism in the apostles' days was by immersion."

Of the government and officers of the primitive churches, these historians give the following testimony:

Waddington.—"In the earliest government of the first christian society, that of Jerusalem, not the elders only, but the whole church were associated with the apostles; and it is even certain that the terms bishop and elder, or presbyter, were in the first instance, and for a short period, sometimes used synonimously, and indiscriminately applied to the same order in the ministry."—History, Page 41.

Again—the same author—"The churches thus constituted and regulated, formed a sort of federative body of independent religious communities, dispersed through the greater part of the empire, in continual communication and constant harmony with each other."

Mosheim.—"The churches of those early times were entirely independent of one another, none of them being subject to any foreign jurisdiction, but each governed by its own rules and its own laws; for though the churches founded by the apostles had this particular deference shown them, that they were consulted in difficult and doubtful cases, yet they had no judicial authority, no sort of supremacy over others, nor the least right to make laws for them. Nothing on the contrary, is more evident than the perfect equality of those primitive churches."

On the officers of the church the same author says: "Let no man confound the bishops of this primitive and golden period of the church with those of whom we read in the following ages; for though they were both distinguished by the same name, yet they differed in many respects. A bishop during the first and second centuries was the person who had the care of one christian assembly, which, at that time, was, generally speaking, small enough to be contained in a private house. In this assembly he acted, not so much with the authority of master as with the zeal and diligence of a faithful servant."

Similar is the testimony of Gibbon.:— "Such was the mild and equable constitution by which the christians were governed for more than a hundred years after the death of the apostles. Every society formed within itself a separate and independent republic; and although the most distant of those little states maintained a mutual as well as friendly intercourse of letters and deputations, the christian world was not yet connected by any supreme authority or legislative assembly."

Similar testimony is borne by Coleman, Neander and Archbishop Whately. Who can fail to see in these descriptions a perfect photograph of the Baptist churches of the nineteenth century.

Of eminent commentators and other Pedobaptist scholars and writers, we have the following:

Doctor Bunson.—"Pedobaptism in the more modern sense, meaning thereby the baptism of infants with the vicarious promises of parents and other sponsors, was utterly unknown to the early church, not only down to the end of the second but even to the middle of the third century."

North British Review.—"Scripture knows nothing of the baptism of infants. There is absolutely not a single trace of it to be found in the New Testament."

Prof. Jacobie.—University of Berlin.—"Infant baptism was established neither by Christ nor his apostles."

Prof. Moses Stewart, Andover.—"There are no commands or plain and certain examples in the New Testamen for the baptism of infants."

Rev. Dr. Woods.—"We have no express precept or example for infant baptism in all the holy writings."

Dr. Augusti, of immersion says:—"I know of no usage of ancient times which seems to be more clearly and certainly made out. I cannot see how it is possible for any candid man, who examines the subject to deny this."

Beza.—"Christ commanded us to be baptised, by which word it is certain immersion is signified. To be baptised in water signifies no other than to be immersed in water."

Whitfield, on Romans 6:4.—"It is certain that in the words of our text, there is allusion to the ancient manner of baptism which was by immersion."

Calvin, on John 3:23 and Acts 8:28.—"From these words it may be inferred that baptism was administered by John and Christ by plunging the body under water."

J. G. Vossius.—"That the Apostles immersed whom they baptised, there is no doubt; and that the ancient church followed this custom is clearly evinced by innumerable testimonies of the fathers."

Dr. Moses Stewart.—"Bapto, baptiso mean to dip, to immerse. All lexicographers and critics of any note are agreed on this."

Martin Luther.—"Baptism is a Greek word and may be translated immersion as when we immerse something in water that it may be completely covered."

Dr. Robert Newton.—"Baptism was originally performed by immersion or dipping the whole body under water to represent the death, burial and resurrection of Christ, and to signify the person's own dying to sin and his resurrection to a new life."

Rev. Dr. Whitby.—"It being so expressly declared here," Romans 6:4, "that we are buried with Christ in Baptism by being buried under water and the argument to oblige us to a conformity to his death being taken hence, and this immersion being religiously observed by all christians for thirteen centuries, it were to be wished that this custom might be again of general use."

Connybare and Howson, on Romans 6:4.—"This passage cannot be understood unless it be borne in mind that the primitive baptism was by immersion."

Dr. Philip Doddridge, on same.—"It seems the part of candor to confess that here is an allusion to the ancient manner of baptising by immersion."

John Wesley, same.—"Alluding to the ancient manner of baptising by immersion." In the old editions of Wesley's journal may be found this entry under date of February 21, 1736. "Mary Welsh, aged eleven, was baptised according to the custom of the first church and the rule of the Church of England by immersion."

Dr. Chalmers.—"The original meaning of the word baptism is immersion; and though we regard it as a matter of indifference whether the ordinance so named be so administered or by sprinkling, we doubt not the prevalent style of administration in the apostles' days was by the actual submerging of the whole body under water."

The late Dr. Charles Anthon, Professor in Columbia college, New York, had the reputation of being the best Greek scholar in America.

On one occasion Rev. Dr. Spring made the statement in public that "baptiso"—the Greek word transferred to our King James' version—signifies to sprinkle and pour. A hearer who heard the statement wrote to Dr. Anthon asking if the statement were true. The following is Dr. Anthon's answer.—"There is no authority whatever for the singular remark of the Rev. Dr. Spring relative to the force of baptiso. The primary meaning of the word is to dip, to immerse; and its secondary meaning, if ever it had any, all refer in some way or another to the same leading idea. Sprinkling and pouring are entirely out of the question."

Of the early Fathers, we have Justin Martyr, Tertullian, Gregory Nazianzen, Cryal of Jerusalem and the "Golden-mouthed Crysostom;" all bearing testimony to the same facts concerning the New Testament churches.

Then there is another class of witnesses who have testified on this question. Where shall we look for the true meaning of words, if not to the lexicons of the language to which the word belongs? For the meaning of a French word we go to a French lexicon. If it be an English, Spanish, or German word, to an English, Spanish or German lexicon. Baptiso is a Greek word, not translated, but simply transferred in our English Testament, and spelled in English letters. On its meaning I have personally consulted Liddell and Scott, Grove, Robinson, Bass, Pickering, Greenfield and Britschneider. These are all standard lexicons and all give the meaning of Baptise, to dip, to plunge, to submerge, to overwhelm. Dr. Stewart said truly: "All lexicographers and critics of any note are agreed on this," that the ancient baptism was by immersion.

Now, if we except Tertullian, whom some Baptist writers claim, with good show of reason, as a Baptist in his belief and practice, none of the above mass of testimony is from Baptist sources. It is from beginning to end, the testimony of learned Pedobaptists who valued their scholarship too highly to misrepresent the truth. I have deemed it best to leave out of this history purely Baptist testimony and confine myself to that furnished by Pedobaptists. Those authors here quoted are among the brightest lights to be found in the Episcopal, Presbyterian, Lutheran, Congregational, and Methodist churches. I mean, of course, aside from the Fathers and those who lived and wrote long before the dawn of the reformation.

If any further proof is needed, it is found in the remains of ancient baptisteries still standing, the paintings and bas-reliefs, which as though kept by Divine power for that purpose, still stand, as ever-enduring witnesses to the methods and practices of Christ's ancient churches.

Here, then, I claim, we have found "the true origin of that sect," which in the fullness of time became known as the Baptist denomination. I ask the reader to take these statements and testimonies, and compare them with the inspired records of those early New Testament churches and he will not only be convinced that the testimonies are true but he will admit that every feature in the photograph of the nineteenth century Baptists is clearly brought out and reproduced in the churches of the New Testament times.

From those churches, then, as a starting point I ask him to follow me along that "Pathway of Fire," as we trace the history of the people holding the same principles, believing the same doctrines, and keeping the ordinances as they were delivered, from the days of the apostles down to the present.

CHAPTER V.

CONTENDING FOR THE FAITH.

"It was needful for me to write you, and exhort you, that you should contend earnestly for the faith once delivered to the saints."

In the present chapter we shall endeavor to explain the causes that led up to the final separation of the early christians into two great bodies, the one going off farther and farther from the truth, until it finally resulted in the great apostasy and the development of the "man of sin," so clearly foretold by Paul; the other pursuing the straight, gospel course though it proved to them a "Pathway of Fire." leading to persecution, to suffering and martyrdom; but which resulted in giving to the generations following that priceless treasure, for which there is no standard of value, freedom to worship God.

Just here arises a most important question. A question which the student must answer before he can rightly appreciate the narrative which will here follow. It is this: In that great separation which gave to the world two such opposite religious bodies, which was right and which was wrong? To this question I shall give no specific answer, but shall leave the reader to render his own answer from a careful study of the facts as I shall give them. I have no doubt, whatever, of the decision of every unprejudiced reader, satisfied not only that he will acquit those early Baptists of all wrong doing, but that he will thank God for that patience and courage which led them to go to their death rather than surrender their God-given right to worship God according to the dictates of his word.

If the reader will glance at the Scripture text with which this chapter is headed, he will see that even in Jude's time, he saw the cloud rising and found it necessary to exhort the brethren "to contend earnestly for the faith." If now he will turn to Paul's Epistles to the Romans, Galatians and Thessalonians he will see how anxious Paul was as he scanned the religious sky and marked the indications of the approaching storm. Standing between Judaism on the one hand and Paganism on the other, and drawing its members from both of these great systems, what wonder if at a very early period, the church should find herself confronted with those errors and abuses so directly opposed to the simplicity of the gospel of Christ. Their fears were well grounded, for scarcely had the apostles closed their life work and sealed their testimony with a martyr's death when those errors and corruptions which they so clearly foresaw began to manifest themselves.

Those errors and corruptions were principally, from three sources. First.—The introduction into their worship of forms and ceremonies not authorized by Christ and his apostles. Judaism sought to combine with the simple methods of the gospel, the forms and ceremonies of the old Mosaic ritual. See Acts 15th. Paganism sought to largely replace the simple act of repentance and faith as a means of salvation with the vain show, the gorgeous ritualism, and sensous practices of Pagan worship, and add to the simple doctrines of the cross, the mysticism and crude generalities of their heathen philosophy.

Second.—The laxity of their discipline and the carelessness of many receiving unconverted and unworthy members into the church. At the first none were admitted but such as gave clear and unmistakable evidence of a genuine change of heart. Then the religion of Christ was unpopular. To be a christian at the first was to deny one's self and take up his cross and follow his Savior, largely through evil report. But when the opposition had subsided and christianity had come to either bask in the smiles or rest under the toleration of worldly power, it became popular to profess to be a christian; and many unconverted people from unworthy motives sought admission into the church. To such members the gorgeous worship and vain philosophy would be more acceptable than the simple faith and forms of the gospel, and resulted still more in narrowing the once clearly defined line between the church and the world.

Third.—The tendency to centralization of

power by which the churches and pastors of
the larger cities, especially Rome, Byzantium
and Carthage, arrogated to themselves, power
and control that was never intended by Christ,
and which formed no place in the early constitution of the churches. This increased more
and more; the other churches and bishops yield-
ing to the power and control of Rome until in
606 the prediction of Paul was fulfilled in the
impious act of making Rome the head of the
church universal, and her bishop the universal
bishop, or the Pope, and declaring him to be
Christ's vice-gerent on earth with power to
control in Christ's room and stead.

It was these innovations and corruptions
which the more spiritual part of the churches,
remembering the admonitions and warnings of
the apostles, so strongly opposed. They
sought earnestly to stem the tide that they
clearly saw, if allowed to flow, would ere long
sweep away the simplicity and purity and spiritual power of the religion of the cross. And
it was these causes—this determination of the
one party to maintain and perpetuate these
innovations, and that of the other to maintain
the purity, discipline and spirituality of the
church that resulted in the final separation and
perpetuating through the ages two great parties
of religionists—the one with its power and
wealth, its prejudices and persecutions, its
gorgeous ritualism, and unholy practices, and
the other with its simplicity and its weakness,
its faithfullness and its sufferings, and its final

triumph in preserving to the world a pure and simple gospel christianity, just as it came from the hands of Christ and his apostles. With this simple statement of facts before him, I ask every intelligent reader: "Which was right and which was wrong?"

It will be readily understood, however, that these innovations and corruptions did not come into the churches all at once;nor did they affect all churches in all sections equally at the same time. All this was of slow growth. The inherent simplicity and purity of the early churches combined with the earnest efforts of that class who opposed those corruptions formed a resisting influence which long stemmed the tide of corruption and made its progress slow. By the year 150 their influence had become such as to awaken the apprehension of many and cause them to sound the alarm. About this period there arose one, Montanus, who by his eloquence and virtue, the simplicity of his doctrines and the purity of his life wielded a mighty influence stemming the tide of corruption in the churches. Montanus had a large following of members, but so far as I can learn, there was no actual separation at this early period. Several writers claim Montanus and his followers as Baptists. The truth is, I think, that they were Baptists in the same sense in which all the churches of the first and part of the second centuries were Baptists. Providence had not yet indicated the point of separation; and Montanus and his followers may be said to represent, not a separate denomination, but the better and more evangelical part of the professed christians, who had not yet so far progressed in corrupting christianity as to make an actual separation necessary.

Still Montanus clearly saw the drift of events and put forth heroic efforts to stem the tide of corruption. Such was his influence and popularity and so numerous were his followers that though imperial decrees were passed against him, they could not be executed.

A hundred years later, however, the point of separation had been reached, and Providence clearly marked out the way. This leads us to consider the direct or immediate cause of the final separation. It is claimed by several church historians that the cause of separation was the election of a bishop. This is only half the truth. The destruction of a ship load of tea in Boston harbor is said to have caused the American revolution. True; but what led up to the destruction of the tea? We must go back of that act, and answer this question, if we get at the real cause of the great struggle for American independence. So, we must go back of that election in Rome in 254 if we would find the real cause of the separation referred to. It will be found in the growing corruption in the latter part of the second and during the third centuries. As God undoubtedly raised up Washington and others to lead the oppressed colonists of America to national freedom, so he raised up men and qualified and called them to the work of maintaining and perpetuating the pure doctrines and practices of the apostolic churches.

In the early part of the third century there was converted at Rome, a pagan philosopher named Novatian. A man of such extensive learning and erudition that Neander classes him among the foremost writers of his age. Was Novatian a christian? I answer—if a deep and pungent conviction of sin, a clear apprehension and acceptance of Christ as a personal Savior, a life of self-sacrifice and consecrated service and a faith and devotion that will lead a man to endure martyrdom rather than surrender his allegiance to his Savior, are evidences of the genuineness of a person's christianity, then Novatian was a christian.

Novatian saw the advancing tide of corruption that was destroying the spiritual life of the churches, and led by the spirit of God, he resolved to stem it at all hazards. In this he was supported by thousands who had long seen and mourned over this sad condition of Christ's kingdom. Meantime the reception of unconverted members, the laxity of discipline, and the constant relapses of apostates back to Paganism, in time of persecution, with their return to the church as soon as the storm blew over, continued.

I quote from Gibbon: "In every persecution there were great numbers of unworthy Christians who publicly renounced their faith, and

who confirmed the sincerity of their abjuration
by the legal act of offering sacrifice to the
Pagan deities. As soon as the severity of the
storm was abated, the doors of the churches
were assailed by the returning multitude, who
solicited with equal ardor, but with varying
success, their re-admission into the the Society
of Christians."

Add to this the growing centralization of
power, the multiplication of sensual forms
and ceremonies, and we have the real cause
which, about the year 254, resulted in that final
separation between those who maintained the
simple apostolic doctrines and practices, on the
one hand, and those who proposed to follow in
the path of corruption, with its vain ceremonies,
its unworthy and unconverted members, and its
gorgeous ritualism and worldly grandeur on the
other. And when that portion of the churches
put forward one Cornelius as the representative of their principles, and elected him bishop
of Rome—those devoted Christians who followed the lead of Novatian said in substance:
"You may do this, and thus persist in your apostasy, but for us we stand on, and by the simple
doctrines and practices of the Gospel, as given
to us by Christ and his apostles." Those worldly minded members persisted. Cornelius was
elected, and thus was taken another step in the
development of the great apostasy, which in
later years became "The Scarlet Woman" of Revelation, who became "Drunk with the blood of
Saints, and the blood of the martyrs of Jesus."

Once more I ask, which was right and which was wrong?

One of the first acts of the Novatian churches was to renounce all intercourse with those churches that they claimed to be apostate, and to refuse to recognize their baptism. They adopted terms of admission into their churches, one of which was as follows: "If you be a virtuous believer and will accede to our confederacy against sin, you may be admitted among us by baptism; or, if a Catholic has baptized you, by re-baptism." For this reason they were called "Anabaptists, or re-baptisers," a name which clung to them and their descendents until 1576 on the Continent, and 1690 in Great Britain, following them, indeed, to America.

"For sixty years those Novatian churches prospered under a Pagan government," so that when Constantine came to the throne in 306, he found churches of that faith and order all over Italy and other parts of his dominions. One of the first acts of this emperor was to try to unite the Novatians and Catholics into one great state church; but those Baptists, true in their allegiance to Christ and his gospel, refused to join in any such unholy alliance. Finding these efforts in vain, Constantine changed his attitude towards them, and inaugurated a most bitter and bloody persecution. Their places of worship were destroyed and their writings burned. Their pastors were imprisoned and some of them put to death. The result was, that, like the persecution at Jerusalem, they became scattered abroad. Some took refuge in France, and carried the gospel with them. Others settled in the valleys of the Piedmont where they afterwards became known as the Voidois or dwellers of the valleys. Still others remained in Italy, hiding from persecution till the storm blew over, so that they may be traced in that country till about 575 when they are lost to sight under the name of the Novatians, only to re-appear later on under other names but still contending for the same doctrines and principles and maintaining the same relations to the churches of the New Testament.

Were those Novatian churches Baptist churches? I answer if the photograph which I have already presented represents the Baptists of to-day, then, in all essential characteristics the Novatians were Baptists; for having due reference to the age in which they lived and to the manner and customs of the people, the world has come to give them credit for bearing a clear cut likeness to the churches of the apostolic age.

Among the many testimonies which I have at hand concerning those Novatian christians I present but one. It is that of Dean Waddington who, in his church history, says of them, "They were stigmatized at the time, both as scismatics and heretics, but they may, perhaps, be more properly considered as the earliest body of ecclesiastical reformers. They arose about the year 250 and subsisted until the fifth century throughout every part of Christendom."

From the disruption of the churches in Italy, let us turn to that of the churches in Africa. In consequence of being further removed from Rome and the influences there, it took longer for the abomination to work among the Africans, than among the Italians. It was not until about the beginning of the fourth century, that the final disruption took place in Africa. Here, too, opposing writers have sought to make it appear that the whole cause of controversy, was the election of the Bishop of Carthage, without consulting the Numidian churches. This does the Donatist Christians great injustice. It was not the election, but the man and the practices, against which they protested.

Cecilian was not only an apostate, but a traitor. When Diocletian demanded that all the scriptures and church records should be given up for destruction, Cecilian, who had them in charge at Carthage, surrendered them to be burned. Against this act an immense number of Christians in Numidia protested; not so much, indeed, against the single act, as against the fearful corruptions of which that act was the representative. They refused all intercourse with those churches that had become so corrupt, and, in Africa, the separation was also complete.

Here, also, we see the hand of God, in raising up men to work out His divine purpose.

. When the necessity arose, God had a man for the place. A man of deep learning, of great purity of life, of burning zeal and firey elo-

quence, and a man mighty in the Scriptures.
Such was the man whom his followers called
"Donatus the Great." Like some mighty rock
he stood in defiance of the advancing wave of
corruption, and when it swept on, it left him
and his mighty host of followers, standing still
firm and true to the principles, doctrines and
practices of the churches of the New Testament.

Such was the influence of this Baptist and his
followers, that, in spite of the opposition of the
corrupt party, and the ban of emperors, in a
few years, the Donatists had churches all over
Africa, until Augustine complained that the
Catholic churches were deserted, and no candi-
dates for their pulpits could be found. On one
occasion they held a conference of pastors, in
which 270, and on another 410 Donatist pastors assembled together. It was largely their
influence and numbers that induced Constantine, when he took the throne, to make the effort to unite them and the Novatians, with the
Catholics, into one great state church. But
those true-hearted Christians, like their brethren in Italy, refused to enter into any such alliance. To all the overtures of Constantine, they
only answered, "What has the Emperor to do
with religion; what have Christians to do at
court?"

Like the Novatians, they refused to recognize the baptism of the Catholics, for which
they, also, were made to bear the reproachful
name of Anabaptists, or rebaptisers.

Like the Novatians, the Donatists were made

to bear the heavy rod of Constantine's persecution. They were scattered—driven from their homes—forced into exile. Their church property was destroyed; their pastors banished, imprisoned, or put to death, and their names cast out as evil. But their torch never went out. Lighted at the altar fires of a pure gospel faith, neither the scorn of an apostate hierarchy, the smiles of emperors, nor the flames of martyrdom could extinguish it. Wherever driven to find a refuge, they carried thence the pure doctrines of the cross—and ere long, its beacon fires were seen shining amid the surrounding darkness, so that long ere their pure gospel light had become extinguished in Africa, in 750 its bright beams had arisen in many of the darkened places of Europe and Asia. It was then that was enacted that scene so graphically described in Revelation, where "The woman fled into the wilderness, to a place prepared for her of God," to which, with other passages referring to the same period, and the same people, I shall ask the attention of the reader in the next chapter.

CHAPTER VI.

THE WILDERNESS WAY.

"And the woman fled into the wilderness where she hath a place prepared for her of God."

In the last chapter we brought the history of our principles down to 575 in Italy, and 750 in Africa. Under the name of Novatians we traced them in the former, and under that of Donatists in the latter country. We saw them persecuted, banished and scattered, but still firm in their allegiance to Christ, and a pure Gospel, taking their wilderness way, with a fortitude and heroism, such as the world seldom witnesses.

It was during this persecution, or about 316, that one Leo, a Christian pastor, took refuge in the valley of Piedmont, when driven from Rome, and it is to him that Archbishop Seysell attributes the rise of the Waldenses. If we accept this as true, we can, at one step, come down the pathway a thousand years, and find our people, but we prefer to follow a longer path, and have a surer road.

The book of Revelation is a wonderful book. There is much of it that I do not understand, and to learn which I will gladly sit at the feet of any who can teach me.

There is some of it, however, that refers so

plainly to the history that we are now tracing, that it is impossible for the careful student to fail to recognize it. Let us study some of these passages.

Turn to Revelation, eleventh chapter, and read the first four verses. Here we have "The Temple, and altar, and them that worship therein; that is the true church, with its members, and its worship, measured or tested, to see if they come up to the standard, and can be relied on when the time of trial comes. "But the court, which is without the Temple"—that is the false professors, those who are Christians in name only, it is useless to measure, for when the testing time comes they will fail. Nothing short of a Christian in deed and in truth, will stand, during those forty and two months, in which the holy city—the true Christians—are to be persecuted and trodden under foot. Forty and two months, of thirty days each, gives us twelve hundred and sixty days, during which this treading is to continue. Turn now to Ezekiel 46, and to Numbers 14:34, and you will find that a symbolic day means a literal year; giving 1260 years as the literal period in which the true church is to be trodden under foot and persecuted.

"And I will give power unto my two witnesses, and they shall prophesy a thousand two hundred and three score days, clothed in sack cloth." The true church will be persecuted and trodden under foot for twelve hundred and sixty years, but her voice shall not be silenced, nor her light hidden. The word here rendered, "witnesses," is the plural form of the Greek word "Marturos," which is only our English word martyr, spelled in Greek characters. "I will give power unto my two martyrs;" and as no two martyrs, even if one should succeed the other, can continue 1260 years, it can only mean that there shall be two lines of martyrs, which, for this space of time shall continue to prophesy, under circumstances of deepest sorrow.

"These are the two olive trees and the two candle sticks"—lamp stands, in the original— "standing before the God of the earth." What is this, but that these two lines of martyrs, these sorrowing, prophesying ones, shall, for 1260 years, be the medium through which the spiritual light of divine truth shall shine upon the earth. The two olive trees standing near indicate that they draw their supplies of light giving power, directly from Christ the fountain head.

Turn now to the 12th chapter and 6th verse. Here we have the woman "fleeing to the wilderness, where she hath a place prepared of God, that they should feed he there a "thousand two-hundred and three score days." That is twelve hundred and sixty years in which she is to remain in the wilderness, where, though trodden under foot and persecuted, she shall still be preserved.

Turn once more to the 14th verse of the same chapter. Here we have the same woman, the true church, "Nourished for a time, times and a half a time." Allowing 360 years as a "time," and multiplying it by three and a half, that is, one time, and two times, and a half a time, and we have 1260 years again, as the period during which God should preserve His true church, even though she should be trodden under foot and persecuted. Her voice should still be heard. Her light should continue to burn. She might prophesy in sackcloth. She might be trodden under foot, but the voice would be heard, and the light continue to gleam, even in the midnight darkness; for

"Truth crushed to earth will rise again,
The eternal years of God are hers;
While error vanquished, writhes in pain,
And dies amid her worshipers."

Now, all this cannot be fortuitous. It was but the hand of God, writing history in advance.

It was but the pencil of God, in the hand of Revelation, drawing the outlines of that picture, whose background would be the darkness of the world's spiritual night, and whose lines and tracings were to be made with the blood of the martyrs of Jesus. Oh, how much is crowded into that brief outline! Twelve hundred and sixty years of sorrow and suffering—of toiling and testimony—of banishment and burning—of faggot and flames—of martyrdom of myriads —of torments and torture, all for the testimony of Jesus, and that there might be preserved to

the generations to come after them, an open
Bible and freedom to worship God.

All hail ye martyred saints! Nearest to the
throne of God, your ransomed souls shall rest.
Through martyr fires ye went to glory and to
God. Up from the flames ye ascended. From
the dark waters, where went out your life—
from the deep cold dungeon, where ye suffered
and pined and died—from the rack, and the secret the place of torture, your souls mounted tri-
umphantly, and angels waited at the gates of
glory, to escort you to the seat of honor nearest
to the throne of God and of the Lamb.

But is there no connection between this picture and the history of our people? Ah, yes!
It is one and the same history. It is twelve hundred and sixty years travel along that "Pathway of Fire," trodden by our fathers, from the
days when they were first scattered by persecution's cruel hand, till the day when God's own
hand brought them forth from the wilderness
that they might lift up their voice like a trumpet. While this scripture lives, let no man say
that Baptist principles became extinct, or that
the light of pure Christianity went out amid the
darkness of the world's spiritual night.

After Constantine had exhausted all his efforts to induce the Novatians and Donatists to
unite with the more corrupt party, and form
one great state church, as stated before, he let
loose the dogs of persecution against them. In
many instances nothing was left but exile or
death. They then became scattered in nearly

all the countries of Europe and Asia. They were soon found in France, Bohemia, Moravia, Bulgaria, Germany, and in the valleys of the Piedmont. Here, under different names, in different localities, they carried on their missionary operations. Patiently toiled and suffered and perished for more than twelve hundred years.

Were these people Baptist? Well they were called "Anabaptists;" and it was for maintaining, in all essential charactristics, the same Bible principles for which Baptists contend now, that they were persecuted, trodden under foot, drowned, beheaded, imprisoned, banished and burned. Yes, in principle, they were Baptists.

This first great scattering under Constantine took place about from 316 to 320. From this point let us look along the "Fiery Pathway" and see if we can find any historical event, which will correspond with our Bible record, and mark the ending of the 1260 years. It should be borne in mind here, that in Bible records, it is only approximate, rather than specific dates that are aimed at.

For many years prior to 1566 the power of the Pope had been weakened in Holland and the Netherlands. Such had been the influence of the Anabaptists that he found it difficult to maintain his standing, and so, in 1566, he resolved on a determined effort to establish the Inquisition in that country. For this work he selected Phillip II of Spain. Phillip entered the Netherlands with a large army, and was met by William, the Silent, the then Prince of Orange, who espoused the cause of the protestants. A long and bloody war followed, which resulted, in about 1579, in the complete defeat of the Spaniards, the entire overthrow of the Inquisition, and severely crippling the power of Rome in all the continent of Europe, and the establishment of the Dutch republic, with William at its head, and freedom to worship God as one of the bassic principles of its government. For these suffering, persecuted Baptists, the 1260 years of prophesying were ended, and, henceforth, in Holland and other parts of Europe, the Anabaptists could find a home where they could worship God according to the dictates of His word. This is largely the explanation of the action of those brethren in England, in sending to Holland, in 1633, where they were certain of finding the "ancient immersion."

Here then, we have one line of martyrs, with the 1260 years clearly defined. Where shall we look for the other line? We will find it across the channel in Britain and Wales. I will not stop definitely to trace it now, as I will take it up later. All I desire to do now is to indicate the two lines of martyrs, so clearly pointed out in the book of Revelation.

Leaving, therefore, the earlier Christians in Britain for further notice, let us, for the present, take up the history at about 430. Up to this period they had been comparatively free from persecution, and had remained comparatively pure. It was about this period, however, that the Picts and Scots invaded Britain and began a fierce and bitter persecution. "As a last resort, for relief from their oppressors, they sent to Decius thrice consul, the groans of the Britains, but obtained no relief." Hoping for aid, they applied to the Anglo-Saxons, only to find them more bitter persecutors and inhuman tyrants than the Picts and Scots. At last, wearied out with their persecutions, some purchased peace with the barbarians, while others, who refused to surrender their allegiance to Christ, sought an asylum in the mountains in Cornwall, and especially in the mountain fastnesses of Wales, where a succession of them can be traced till the Reformation. Here, also, the women found a home in the wilderness.

Adding now to this date—430, the 1260 years referred to in Revelation, and where does it bring us? To 1690. What great event, bearing on this question, occurred then? It is true that, previous to that, the so-called reformation in England had been established; but it brought no liberty of conscience to the despised Anabaptists. The fires of Smithfield burned and the prison doors still swung to admit them. But in 1690 William and Mary were crowned king and queen of England. One of their first acts was to secure toleration in all matters of religion—an act that, to this day, is known as "England's Magna Charta." This was followed by the battle of the Boyne, by which the persecuting power of Rome was forever broken. The

1260 years for the other line of martyrs was ended.

Here then we have the two distinct lines of martyrs, who, according to the prediction of the Apocalyptic seer, kept alive the lamp of Divine truth, through suffering and persecution for 1260 years, while the scarlet clothed women was "drunken with the blood of the saints, and with the blood of the martyrs of Jesus." To trace more closely those martyred saints, along their "Pathway of Fire," will form the subject of future chapters.

CHAPTER VII.

WITNESSING IN SACKCLOTH.

"Here is the patience of the Saints. Here are they that keep the commandments of God, and the faith of Jesus."

The thirteenth verse of the fourteenth chapter of Revelation, has always been to me, a very instructive and comforting portion of Scripture. Like other ministers, I have regarded it as teaching the blessedness of the righteous, after death, and it has been a favorite text for funeral sermons, of those who died in Christ. I have no doubt now but it teaches this blessed truth. Lately, however, I have come to regard it as having specific reference to those who, according to the verse preceding it, placed at the head of this chapter, had "kept the commandments of God, and the faith of Jesus," during those dark and trying periods, when the earth was made to drink of the blood of the saints.

It is a fact, as important as true, that "the occasion develops the man," whether the occasion be political or religious. This is only another way of saying, that when God wants a man for a specific purpose, he knows where to find him. This was true of Paul, of Luther, and of Washington; and it was equally true of those whom God raised up, through all those dark and gloomy ages, as waymarks in the wilderness—or as kindling wood to keep the altar fires still burning.

About the year 653—a hundred years before the Donatists became extinct, there was converted in Armenia, one of those men, undoubtedly chosen of God, for his own great purpose. His name was Constantine; and his conversion illustrates most clearly the fact above stated. A Baptist deacon, who it is said, had been a prisoner among the Saracens, was traveling through Armenia, and was entertained at Constantine's home—some authorities say, through a fit of illness. In return for his kindness, he presented Constantine with two manuscript rolls, containing the epistles of Paul. Constantine read them and was converted. He at once threw away his Manichaean books and became a flaming herald of the simple Gospel of Jesus. So closely did he and his converts follow the teachings of Paul, that they became known as Paulicians.

It was in Armenia that the Novatians and Donatists had done much of their missionary work; and at the time of Constantine's conversion they had become very numerous under the local name of "Bogomiles," or "Men of Prayer."

Constantine drew his theology directly from the word; but when he came to compare his views with those of the "Bogomiles he found them to agree with his own.—Bible truth is always consistent with itself—and so, in a short time, he became a very prominent leader among them, knowing no creed but that of Christ and Paul. This fact accounts for the immense numbers of Paulicians. They were not all converts of Constantine and his successors, but the Paulicans and Bogomiles, were in principle, one and the same people. So numerous were they that, when that fiend incarnate, the Empress Theodora, had cruelly martyred one hundred thousand of them, they were still " like the leaves of the forest."

The Paulicians were truly missionary in spirit and effort. They carried out the great commission to preach the gospel to every creature. They sent out their missionaries, two by two, "everywhere preaching the word." The result was that, in spite of the edicts of the kings, the fiery opposition of the Greek and Roman churches, and the martyrdom of many, in a hundred years they were numbered by hundreds of thousands, not only in Armenia, but in "the regions beyond."

In 741 Emperor Constantine V banished very many of them to Thrace, whence they carried the gospel into Bulgaria, resulting in the conversion of many thousand Bulgarians.

From 775 to 815 the Paulicians were almost constantly the subjects of severe persecution; but from the latter date till about 830 foreign wars attracted the attention of the Emperors, and they had rest. This was only the prelude to still greater suffering. Theophilus died, leaving the crown to his son Michael, only five years of age. Theodora became regent, and, filled with hatred of the Paulicians, resolved on nothing short of their extermination. Her first act was to issue a decree, requiring all her subjects to conform to the worship of the Greek church. This the Paulicians refused, when she sent an immense army with instructions to put to death all, both high and low, who refused to obey her decree. The scene of carnage and death went on till between one and two hundred thousands of those Paulician Baptists had sealed their allegiance to Christ with their blood.

Just here permit me to state a fact that has forcibly impressed me. I have recently been investigating, somewhat, the Armenian massacres in the same land, where dwelt, a thousand years ago, those Paulician and Bogomile christians, and where fell those more than a hundred thousand martyrs. I have been impressed with the testimony of even their enemies, to the purity of life—the humbleness of walk, the simplicity of manners, and nearness to Bible teachings, of those Armenian christians. They have no connection with either the Greek or Roman church, or the Mohammedans. They are a body of christians by themselves. They do not worship saints. They believe in the independence of the churches. They have no priests, but simple pastors. They believe in spiritual christianity and baptize only by immersion. When we remember all the changes through which they have passed, the influence brought to bear and the persecutions endured, amid all of which they have remained true to the simpler doctrines and practices of the early christians, it would seem as though those early Paulician Baptists had left an impress, that all the ages have been unable to obliterate. Here is a subject worthy of the most careful study of our Baptist historians.

Returning to our history. The converts to the Paulician faith in Bulgaria were known as Bulgarians, from the place whence they came, and they can be traced to the fifteenth century.

As those Paulicians form one of the most numerous and interesting sects of all of those early Baptists, and as they form a sort of connecting link between those who preceded them and those who come after, it will be well to pause at this point in our pathway, and convince ourselves still further of their Baptistic sentiments.

From a careful study of their doctrines, as given by Mosheim and others, it is apparent that the following will about cover the ground of their doctrinal belief:

1. They believed in the personal piety of all church members. None but converted people should be allowed to join the church.

2. They rejected all sacraments as a means of salvation—accepting them only as symbols of religion and commands of Christ.

3. They totally rejected infant baptism.

4. They refused to worship images, or to accept the teachings of the Greek or Catholic churches concerning them.

5. They refused the Roman idea of the priesthood, and abhored the confessional.

6. They denied the doctrine and duty of penance, and bitterly denounced the idea of purgatory.

7. Their only baptism was the immersion of a believer in water, on his profession of faith in Christ.

"The Paulicians sincerely condemned the memory and opinions of the Manichaean sect, and complained of the injustice of impressing that invidious name on the simple followers of Paul and of Christ. The objects which had been transformed, by the magic of superstition, appeared to the eyes of the Paulicians in their genuine and naked colors. They attached themselves with peculiar devotion to the writings and character of Paul, in whom they gloried. In the gospels and epistles of Paul, Constantine investigated the creed of the primitive christians, . . . and the words of the gospel were, in their judgment, the baptism and communion of the faithful—Gibbon.

Dr. Allix, who made a careful study of them, says—"They, with the Manichaeans"—mark, he does not say that they were Manichaeans—"were Anabaptists, or rejectors of infant baptism.

Dr. Milner says of them—"They were simply scriptural in the use of the sacraments; they were orthodox in the doctrine of the Trinity; they knew of no other mediator than the Lord Jesus Christ."

Dean Waddington, after carefully investigating all the charges brought against them by their enemies, gives this testimony: "They"— the charges—"evince their freedom from some of the popular superstitions of the Greeks—adoration of the virgin, and reverence for the fancied relics of the cross; and this again had been crime sufficient to arm against them, in the eighth and ninth centuries the intemperate zealots of the Oriental church. Add to this that they held images of the saints in no reverance, and recommended to every class of people the assiduous study of the Sacred Word; not suppressing their indignation against the Greeks, who closed the sources of divine knowledge to all except the priests, and we shall not wonder that the Paulicians became the victims of the most disgraceful persecution that ever disgraced the Eastern church."

With such testimony as the above, I am surprised to note that Dr. Vedder in his "Short History of the Baptists," classes the Paulicians with the Manichaeans. The truth is—with due reference to the times and age, the manners and customs of the people among whom they lived, they may be reasonably counted among the Baptist descendants from the apostolic churches.

We have thus traced the history of New Testament church principles along the pathway of time, from that little church at Jerusalem. We have followed the principles, and found them prominent among the Novatians of Italy, the

Donatists of Africa, and the Paulicians of Armenia. Here we have reached the middle of the eleventh century. The whole pathway has been, more or less, a pathway of fire and persecution, through which hundreds of thousands have gone up to glory and to God, in chariots of literal flame. Still, the voice has not been silenced, the lamp has not been extinguished.

Ere we leave them, to take our journey further along this "Fiery Pathway," let us take one swift glance at the field of their labors, and gain strength and inspiration to follow them amid still darker persecutions, and by the light of still fiercer fires, through which our pathway must lead. The place is Armenia, amid the graves of the hundreds of thousands of our brethren. The time is the middle of the eleventh century. "We stand on that sublime height of Ararat, from which Noah looked down on the receding waters of the deluge as they drew back from hill and dale, and once more the earth appeared in view." Alas! another deluge covers the earth. It is the darkness of spiritual night. It is the beginning of the darkest period of the Christian dispensation. Around us, and to the north, the beast of the sea, the Greek hierarchy is pouring out his floods of persecution to destroy the saints. To the south, where rise the tall minerets of the "Seven Hilled City" sits on her throne of state, the Scarlet woman, the Roman hierarchy, already becoming "drunken with the blood of the saints, and with the blood of the martyrs of Jesus."

But look! Another scene appears, as if to tell us that the imperishable truth of God still lives, and that the blessed light of ages still shines, here and there, in the midst of this almost impenetrable darkness. The torch lighted at the fire of Christ's own altar, is not yet extinguished. By its beams we can take a retrospect of the past, and, peering out into the darkness, see and read "the waymarks in the wilderness," pointing out our pathway in the future. Just below us lies the sacred land, long ago trodden by the feet of the Son of God. There, in "the vale of Kedron," with Olivet guarding her, like a faithful sentinel, reposes the "City of Zion," whence first beamed forth the effulgent light of the Gospel truth. Away to the west, under the very shadows of the Vatican, is seen the glimmering light, which, like the burning bush on Horeb's plain, burns but is not consumed. Yonder, beyond the blue waters of the Mediterranean, lies Africa, whose soil has been made sacred by the blood of the martyred Donatists. Still yonder, where rise the towering summits of the lofty Alps, is seen another light, where the fleeing woman has found a "home in the wilderness, prepared for her of God." At their base sleeps the beautiful valley of the Piedmont, and there, also, have the children of the King found a refuge from their oppressors, and there "the green foliage of the tree of life" is sending forth its budding leaves for the healing of the nations. Beyond it still, where tower those lofty summits of the Pyrenees, the scattered Baptists of Italy and Africa, still bearing the reproachful name of "Anabaptist," and still firm in their allegiance to Christ and his truth, calmly wait for the bursting of that storm, the mutterings of whose distant thunders we can hear as we look down from the summit of Ararat. Still further to the west, beyond the dancing billows of the English channel, where rise those chalky cliffs of that "Seagirt Isle," in the fastnesses of those mountains of Wales, "we can see the light shining above the hills," and we know the altar fires of a living faith are burning there also. Surely we need not despair however intense the darkness, when around us, on every hand, "the lights along the shore" are still so brightly burning.

But we have lingered long, as from our lofty summit we have taken this survey of the situation, let us down and away once more as we look along the Fiery Pathway for the footprints of our fathers.

CHAPTER VIII.

CAST DOWN BUT NOT DESTROYED.

"And I saw the woman drunken with the blood of the saints and the blood of the martyrs of Jesus."

The introduction of christianity was the signal for persecution. Scarce had the Son of God made his advent to earth when the devil marshalled his hosts against him. His infant life was only preserved by miraculous interposition and his manhood was one long scene of suffering and reproach which finally closed on a cruel Roman cross. His disciples one after another sealed their testimony with martyrdom. The heroic Paul after leaving the sorrowful record in the eleventh of the Second Corinthians went to Rome and died a martyr's death. Thus was christianity launched amidst the billows of the world's hatred and from that time till now have clouds and storms been round about her. Other things being equal the nearer the followers of Jesus have kept to his commandments, the wilder the storms have raged.

Thus far, as we have seen, the altar fires, kindled by Christ and fanned by the Holy Spirit have remained unextinguished. We have seen their light shining all along the pathway down to the middle of the eleventh century. From hence, though they shone none the less clearly, we shall find the efforts to extinguish them redoubled.

One fact is encouraging. We have reached a point where the light of history shines more clearly. Facts are more fully attested. The records are more extensive. Perhaps, were all the history written, from the first to about the eleventh century, it would be found that the martyrs for Jesus were as numerous in those centuries as in those that followed. Indeed, the half has never been written in any age and the present generation will never know, till they learn it in the other world, all that it has cost in human suffering and martyrdom to secure to them what they now enjoy in freedom to worship God.

But where shall we next look for the footprints of our fathers? We will let Gibbon, the historian answer.

"It was in the country of the Albegeois in the Southern Province of France that the doctrines of the Paulicans were most deeply implanted. In the practice, or at least in the theory of the sacraments, the Paulicians were inclined to abolish all visible objects of worship and the words of the gospel were, in their judgment, the baptism and communion of the faithful."

Again.—"They conversed freely with strangers and natives and their opinions were silently propagated in Rome and the kingdoms beyond the Alps. It was soon discovered that many thousands of Catholics of every rank and either sex had embraced their heresy."

Still further.—"In the busy age of the Crusades some sparks of curiosity and reason were kindled in the western world. The heresy of Bulgaria, the Paulician sect, was successively transplanted in Italy and France."

From the above statements of Gibbon it can be seen how easily we can trace the principles we are following from Armenia and Bulgaria to France and Italy, even if there were no other footprints save those that were made by the Paulician Baptists. But let us precede them and look among the inhabitants of Italy and France and in the mountains and valleys that make up the country of the Alps, the Appennines and the Pyrenees and see if there were no Baptists there to greet them before the Crusaders took up their march towards, not the tomb of Jesus, but of Joseph of Arimathaea.

Gibbon says the Paulicians were most deeply implanted in the country of the Albegeois. This was the home to which the early christian principles had already been carried.

The light kindled by the Novatians in Italy had never been totally extinguished. In secret places those early Baptists have worshipped God, and kept the fire burning. Hidden away were kept some "live coals from off the altar," ready to be fanned into a flame, whenever God's own time would come. So when the

Paulicians carried their doctrines into Italy and France and Spain, they found the soil prepared, the leaven already working.

How did that gospel get there? For answer go back to the early part of the fourth century, when the floodgates of persecution were opened on the defenseless Novatians and Donatists. "The woman fled to the wilderness," to this very place "prepared for her of God." It was those persecuted Anabaptists that God had in his mind, when he created those mountain fast-nesses and those secluded valleys. It was to these they fled and it was they who planted the first seeds of the gospel there, and they found a fertile soil. In a comparatively short time, such was their piety and zeal, they were numbered by hundreds of thousands. The valley of Piedmont and other portions of France and Spain was their natural home. From there they sent missionaries to Holland, Switzerland, Bohemia, and Germany. So great was their success, that, by the beginning of the twelfth century, one of their number could travel over a large part of Europe and be entertained at the home of one of their brethren every night.

During the crusades of the eleventh and twelfth centuries, the attention of Popes and Kings was turned toward the "Holy Sepul-chre;" and, like the early apostolic christians, it can be said: "Then had the churches rest, and walking in the fear of the Lord were multiplied."

In the beginning of the thirteenth century, the storm broke in all its fury. The crusades had ended, and had largely proved a failure. Pope Innocent III now turned all his attention to the extermination of the defenseless Anabaptists. A general crusade was proclaimed, the field of battle offering better prospect of success. Indulgencies were sold to raise money to carry on the war of extermination. Then began a scene that presents the blackest page in all the book of history. Those inoffensive and defenseless people became the victims of Rome's bitterest vengence, and an indiscriminate slaughter was begun. Vast armies were sent out with instructions only to destroy and exterminate.

Count Raymond of Toulouse sought to shield such as were in his dominions, but all in vain. Before that mighty wave of cruelty, every barrier gave way and the valleys and streams, the hills and streets ran red with martyr blood. "The woman was drunken with the blood of the Saints and with the blood of the martyrs of Jesus." It was this scene that drew from the poet Milton those touching lines:

"Avenge, O Lord thy slaughtered saints of old,
Whose bones lie bleaching on the Alpine mountains cold
Even those who kept thy truth so pure of old,
Forget not. In thy book let all their names be written."

Says the British Encyclopedia:—"The bloody war of extermination which followed has scarcely a parallel in history. As town after town was taken, the inhabitants were put to the sword without distinction of age or sex; the ecclesiastics who were in the army being especially blood thirsty." "Slay all, God will know his own," was the battle cry, and, like demons, did the fanatical religionist soldiers respond to it. No man can estimate the great number slain, but their names are all preserved and their martyr crowns will point them out in that day. (See Rev. 6:9.)"

But were they exterminated? No. Although this war had been carried on for twenty-five years, at its close, "the blood of the martyrs had so become the seed of the church" that fully 800,000 of those Baptists still remained in various parts of Europe.

History has established one fact, viz: The scattering method is the poorest method for exterminating Baptist principles. Sixteen centuries of experience has proven this fact beyond a doubt and the twenty-five years of effort to scatter and exterminate those Albigenses, and other sects professing the same principles was no exception to the rule. It only sowed the seed more broad cast; and we trace it to Switzerland, to Holland, to Germany, and everywhere, like fire in the forest, each enkindling grew until the light of all blended into one great flame.

We must now, for a few moments, turn our attention to denominations, called by other names, but holding the same principles. Of these we shall have time only to speak of their great leaders and give a passing glance at their history. The first of these is

PETEO DE BRUIS,

whose followers were called Petrobrussians. The name and memory of this heroic man will live while there are people on the earth, who love an open Bible, a pure church and a living faith. "A burning and a shining light," he carried the torch of truth, until it fell from his nerveless grasp amid the martyr fires in which his heroic soul mounted up to the throne of God and the Lamb. He fell at his post, being burned at the stake in 1126. His followers became numerous and may be traced in various parts of Europe, till the year 1300.

Another name that stands out, like a bright beacon light, in the darkness, is

HENRY OF LAUSAUNE.

In the old city of Toulouse Henry first lifted up his voice like a trumpet to show the people their sins; but he was only permitted to live long enough to set in motion a reform that would still live after its promoter had gone to take the martyr's crown. Driven from Toulouse, he fled to the mountains, but was hunted like a fox, brought back and thrown into a loathsome dungeon, where he was left to languish and die. No voice comes to us from that lone dungeon, no records are kept of his anguish, while pining slowly to death for Jesus' sake, but among the immortals up yonder, Henry of Lausanne appears wearing a martyr's crown.

"Henry was a Baptist, believing in the Spirituality of Christs' kingdom, the supreme authority of Christ as King, and the immersion of true believers."—Ford.

His followers were called Henricians and may be traced for several years.

Still another name that is imperishable, and that will shine with ever increasing lustre, as the ages roll on, is

ARNOLD OF BRESCIA.

His followers were known as Arnoldists and had their origin about 1137. As a distinct body, they can be traced but a few years after the death of their intrepid leader, when they no doubt, became incorporated into other bodies, holding the same principles. When he was being pursued, he went boldly to Rome and in defiance of the entire Papacy, dared to proclaim the simple gospel story, four hundred years before Luther nailed his thesis to the doors of his church.

"He was a Baptist and for holding just what Baptists now hold, he was arrested, condemned, crucified, and then burned and his ashes thrown into the Tyber." Ford.

If the act of Luther, in defying the council at Wirms, has rendered his name immortal, what honor should be given to that intrepid reformer, "Arnold of Brescia," for his mighty courage, his lofty purpose, and his sublime faith, in leaving his place of sheltered security, and in defiance of the whole power of the Vatican, lifting up his voice even in the "seven hilled city," and

"Like a gate of steel,
Fronting the sun, receives and renders back
His figure and his heat."

Ah! It was because such heroic reformers had preceded Luther and Calvin and Knox that they were able to make the reformation a success. All honor to their memory for their heroism and courage, and the faith that sustained them in that mighty conflict by which the chains were broken and the Bible made free. Not one leaf would we pluck from the laurel crown their memory wears. But shall we not have some recognition for the same act, under much more adverse circumstances? The world, aye, and the church too, while they are loud in their praise of Luther, are slow to speak of those God honored Baptists who purchased soul liberty with their lives. But the world is beginning to recognize their conflicts and their triumphs; and in after years the world's justification and the church's gratitude will form a monument to their memory and heroic deeds that will speak their praise,

"When gems and monuments and crowns
Shall blend in common dust."

It will be well at this point, that the reader may follow us more intelligently, to give a short description of the geographical location of some of the religious bodies to which I am now to refer.

The Pyrenees mountains form the boundary line between France and Spain; extending from near the Bay of Biscay on the west to the Mediterranean sea. The Albigenses were mostly settled on the North, or French side of the mountains and the Waldenses on the South, or Spanish side. In their principles and doctrines at the time here referred to they were practically the same; their names indicating local rather than doctrinal differences. Indeed, the same people would sometimes be called by one name and sometimes by another. It was not uncommon for the Albigenses, when persecutions would become unbearable, to cross the mountains and find a refuge with their brethren in Spain till the storm would subside. When Spain would come down with persecution, the Waldenses would take refuge in France. The reader must remember that "history travels slowly;" and that of those people cover several hundred years. It is true, that in later years, some of the Waldenses inclined somewhat to Pedobaptism; but so far as the history of the Albigenses can be traced, this was not the case with them. The Albigenses retained their distinctive Baptist sentiments; and it is from these through the Lollards that we trace the line of our principles to England where they

continued to suffer persecution till the act of
toleration relieved them.

The Alps is a range of mountains, dividing
the Southeastern part of France from Italy
and the Appenines lie between Italy on the
South and France and Switzerland on the
north. Lying at their base, and sheltered by
them on the north and west is the beautiful
valley of the Piedmont, and the Province of
Lombardy. This is an immense table-land,
terminating in wide valleys extending far up
in the mountains, forming a thousand nooks
and shelters, and sequestered spots, where
fertile vales, crystal waters, the richest soil and
healthiest climate combine to constitute one
of the most delightful spots on earth. When
God created the world he looked along down
the ages, and knowing the future as the
present, here he prepared the place to which
his persecuted church could flee when the storm
of persecution should break on her defenseless
head. No spot could be found under the broad
sky, more evidently designed, as a place of
refuge where, unmolested, his people could
pursue their peaceful avocations and at the
same time preserve to the world the priceless
treasure of a pure gospel. So, when the storm
broke and the tempest of persecution raged
against his pure church, he placed a guide-
board pointing to "the place prepared for her
of God," and with a firm faith those Novatian
and Donatist Baptists turned their steps
towards this sheltered land. Leo and his com-

panions,— how many we will never know—
came and planted the seeds of truth and here
they lived and toiled, and "kept the faith."
Known simply as "Voidois, or dwellers in the
valley," their innocent ways, pure lives, and
simple gospel commended them to all. From
here they sent forth their pastors, or bards, self-
sacrificing missionaries of the cross with their
pack of merchandise on their shoulders and
the Gospel of Jesus in their hearts. Out on
Italy's broad field they planted it, and erelong
we have a host of "Paterines,"so named because
of their patient endurance of persecution.
Across the Alps, in the sunny soil of Southern
France, and lo, the Albigenses, from Albi, their
principle seat, are numbered by the thousands.
Farther still and the sunny slopes of Spain, at
the base of the Pyrenees, are made a moral
garden where the flowers of a pure christianity
bud and bloom. Still on, climbing "the
steeps of Appennines," and Switzerland and
Germany receive the blessed results of their
missionary work. On, still on, and Holland
and the Netherlands re-echo back the glad
accents of Salvation. Menno Simon catches
the inspiration of a true faith, and, "like a
mighty force let loose," he goes forth, lifting
high the banner of the cross, and soon the name
of "Mennonite" or Dutch Baptist becomes a
household word. And so, we have the Voidois
of the valleys, the Paterines of Italy, the
Waldenses of Spain, the Mennonites of Holland, the Anabaptists of Switzerland and the

German Baptists of Germany all bearing different names, locally, but all alike in every essential characteristic, and all bearing the closest resemblance to the Paulicians of Armenia, the Donatists of Africa, the Novatians of Italy, the gospel churches of Jerusalem and Palestine, and the Baptists of the United States. It is not the name, but the doctrines of the New Testament that constitute one common chain that binds them together through all the ages. Principles, not names, has ever been the Baptist watchword.

But how shall we account for this close resemblance of principles betwen all those numerous bodies here named and the early Donatists, and Novatians? Two facts will furnish the answer and the only satisfactory answer that can be given. First.—the former were the literal descendants of the latter; and second, they all alike drew their oil from the same source—the "Spirit and the Word," represented by "the two olive trees" in Revelation. The Bible teaches the same truth to all.

In Switzerland and Germany the Baptists continued till the reformation; and when first its light dawned on the latter, thousands of the German and Swiss Baptists came forth to offer their sympathy and aid to Luther in his great work. Indeed from all over Europe, they rose, like Ezekiel's dry bones in the valley, believing that the day of their deliverance had come; thus fully substantiating the statement of Mosheim, that "Before the rise of Luther and

Calvin, they lay concealed in almost all the countries of Europe."

Let us now turn to Holland. It was in1492 the year made memorable by the discovery of the New World, that an event occurred of scarcely less importance, viz: the birth in Friesland of Menno Simon. He was educated in the church of Rome and became a Roman priest. While studying the sacred word, he became convicted of sin, and savingly converted. About this time he read of the martyrdom of one Snijder, "who was beheaded, his body torn on the wheel and his bodiless head set on a stake, as a warning to all others not to be guilty of his crime." And what heinous crime, reader, think you that it was? The court record says, it was "For being rebaptised, and persevering in that baptism." This settled the question with Menno. From that moment he became a zealous preacher of the same faith, and continued, his field being all Europe, till his death in 1559. Twenty years after his death Holland became a free government, with liberty of conscience, in matters of religion. The very close relation between the Baptists of Holland, and the later Baptists of England I will show further on. I will close this chapter with the testimony of Cardinal Hosius, himself a Roman Catholic, and president of the Council of Trent. He says: "If the truth of religion were to be judged of by the readiness and cheerfulness which a man of any sect shows in suffering, then the opinions and persuasions of no sect can be truer or surer, than those of the Anabaptists; since there have been none for these twelve hundred years past that have been more previously punished." When was this statement made? In 1570. Deduct 1260 years, and we are carried back to the days of the Novatians and Donatists. Surely God must have forced this testimony, to help explain the vision of the seer, where he saw the woman fleeing to the wilderness. It is well to bear in mind that the flight of the woman does not refer to a single specific date, as much as to an act; and, indicates simply that pure christianity would be trodden under foot, and its professors would be compelled to flee to their hidden places, and seek a refuge where they could worship God in secret. Put this statement of Vossius with that of Mosheim, the "True of origin of the Baptists is hidden in the remotest depths of antiquity"—and that "Before the rise of Luther and Calvin they lay concealed in nearly all the countries of Europe," and we are led to ask, what more evidence can be demanded, to convince the christian world of the ancient origin of the Baptists?

CHAPTER IX.

OUT OF GREAT TRIBULATION.

"These are they that have come out of great tribulation."

Having now traced the one line of martyrs, the Baptists on the continent, down to the reformation, let us leave them, while we go back and trace the other line in Great Britain and Wales. This we shall be compelled to do very briefly, to keep our little book within the prescribed limits.

Just when, or how, christianity was first planted in Britain we do not know. The native Britains were Druids; but, at a very early period, certainly in the first century, the gospel was carried there, and many of the natives were converted. The groves, where once had been offered the bloody worship of the Druids, were made to re-echo the praises of the once Crucified Christ.

For the first three centuries, the churches of Britain seem to have remained comparatively pure. The distance from the contentions and influences which affected the change in Italy and Africa was in their favor; so that at the beginning of the fourth century, no special fault could be found with the doctrines and practices of the churches of that country.

In the very early part of the fifth century, the Picts and Scots invaded Britain, overran the country and began a course of severe perse-

cution. Decius was appealed to, but found it
impossible to afford the Britains relief. The
Anglo-Saxons, were then appealed to, who
responded so fully that they drove back the
Picts and Scots, overran the country and took
possession of it themselves.

They soon became more tyrannical and cruel
in their persecution than the others. At length
worn out with constant persecution, and rendered defenseless by their enemies, some of the
christians renounced their religion and made
peace with the barbarians. Others, and there
were many of them, refused to surrender their
religion and fled to the mountains, especially
the mountain fastnesses of Wales, and the
country in and around Cornwall, where they
might worship God in peace according to the
dictates of His word.

The Anglo-Saxons, having gained full control
of the country, they erelong became an object
of great interest to the Roman Catholics and
they resolved to undertake their conversion to
the Catholic faith. A monk named Austin
was persuaded to undertake the mission and
he and his co-workers reached England in
the latter part of the fifth century.

Their instruction was, not to preach Christ
and him crucified as the way of salvation, but
to adapt his religion, so far as possible to the
customs of the barbarians, and thus win them
by craft. He presented letters of introduction
to the Saxon King, who was pleased with the
manners and address of the crafty monk and

was finally persuaded to be baptised in the
Catholic faith. This paved the way for
Austin's success, and, erelong there were thous-
ands of Catholic converts, and the rivers
became the scenes of baptism of multitudes.
The only mode of course was immersion.

Having thoroughly established the Roman
Catholic religion among the Anglo-Saxons,
Austin next turned his attention to the conversion of the Welsh christians. Here, however,
he found different material. He found a people already rooted and grounded in the truth.
A people who knew the difference between a
vain ceremony and a living faith. They refused
either to receive his doctrine or to obey his
mandate. They were ready to accept and to
obey as far as their duty to do so was shown
them from God's word.

A conference was finally arranged between
Austin and some of the Welsh pastors.
These latter explained that they could do
nothing without consulting their churches—
the strongest evidence that, at least, they
possessed one of the most prominent of Baptist
doctrines, the perfect equality of pastor and
people. It was finally agreed to call a council
and give Austin an opportunity to submit his
propositions. The council assembled in a grove
of oaks. In glowing terms Austin set forth the
advantages they would derive from embracing
the Catholic faith and then submitted his propositions. These were found to be so at
variance with their ideas of the Bible that the

Welsh christians at once refused even to consider them. The wily monk then began to yield one demand after another, until, at last, he insisted on only three propositions. These were:

First.—That they should acknowledge the authority of the pope.

Second.—That they should keep easter like Catholics.

Third.—That they should baptise their children.

To all these propositions those Welsh Baptists gave a most positively negative answer.

At last the patience of the poor monk was exhausted; and "changing his countenance toward them," he cried in great anger: "Well since ye will not have peace and quietness, ye shall have woe and wretchedness."

And truly, indeed, did Austin carry out his threats. The Saxon barbarians, recently converted to Catholicism, without religious intelligence, change of heart or grace, were only a set of religious fanatics and ready to do the bidding of the lords of their conscience. With a zeal, worthy of a nobler course, they began the work of destruction. The college at Bangor, a noble seat of learning, was destroyed, the preachers were put to death, and over two thousand martyrs sealed their testimony with their lives. The residue fled to the mountains, where they gathered up their scattered breth-

ren and again laid the foundation of their work
for Christ and His churches.

Though cast down they were not destroyed.
In spite of all the fiery opposition, these Welsh
Baptists kept the lamp of truth burning,
through all the ages of darkness and when the
bright beams shone from the hill tops of France
and Spain and Italy and Germany, they were
answered back from the chalky cliffs beyond
the blue waters that separate Britain from the
rest of Europe.   It was indeed a place prepared
of God, where the light of a pure christianity
might shine, while so much of the world was
enveloped in spiritual darkness.

All the evidence at command goes to prove
that these Welsh christians, in all essential
characteristics were Baptists.   An old Welsh
chronicle says:—

> "And thus they dwelt here
> An hundred and fifty year,
> So that never christening
> Came here to be known in the land,
> Nor bell ringing nor church hallowed
> Nor child was there baptised."

Following down the fiery pathway of those
Welsh Baptists, we come to some of the most
illustrious names to be found in the annals
of the country. We might mention William
Tyndale, who gave England the Bible in her
own language, and had already got the four
books of Moses into Welsh before exchanging

the cross for a crown. Lewellyn Tindale, Hesekiah Tindale, Howell Vaugn, who stood with towers of truth on the Rock of Ages, while like billows of persecution and error broke around them. Of Walter Brute, that staunch Baptist, who when arrested and brought before the ecclesiastics, and required to give a written answer, wrote these sublime words:—

"In the name of Father, Son, and Holy Ghost I, Walter Brute, sinner, layman, husbandman, and christian, having been accused to the bishop, that I did err in matters of christian faith, do answer, if any man, of any sect, will show that I err, by the authority of the sacred scriptures, I will gladly receive his information."

When the reformation dawned in England, the Welch Baptists came out of there "Piedmont of Wales," from the vale of Carleon, from the valleys and recesses of those Welch Alps, Merthyn and Tydfyl, where all the long centuries they had cherished the faith received from their fathers. They were joined by many reformers from England, who, no doubt, brought with them some of the lesser errors of their cast off church, notably mixed communion; but the Welsh Baptists had never imbibed this error. Even to the present day, there are to be found no truer Baptists than are to be found in Wales.

LOLLARD AND WICKLIFFE.

To write any kind of a history of Baptist principles in England and not mention Lollard and Wickliffe, would be to write Hamlet and leave Hamlet out.

It was about 1320 that the Albegensian faith was successfully transplanted into England. Walter Reynard, called Lollard, by way of reproach, as claimed by some, was the instrument chosen of God, for that grand missionary enterprise. We can only account for the result in one of two ways. Either there were thousands of people of the same faith who stood ready to greet and join Lollard in his work, or he must have had special enduement of the Holy Spirit. Possibly it may have been both combined. So numerous did they become that Newberry, in his history of England, declares them to be "As numerous as the sands of the sea."

Did I wish to write a large volume, I could find ample material, in the persecutions of the Lollards and Wickliffites, but I must pass them, with the briefest reference. Lollard himself was burned and his followers cruelly persecuted for holding the same views the Baptists do today. Let the "Lollards' Tower," standing there on the banks of the Thames, remain, a silent and gloomy witness to the tortures and persecutions of the Lollards, and of the final triumph of truth. What was their crime? It was that they refused to exchange the commandments of the Bible for the bulls of Popes, or the traditions of Rome. For this William Somter was arrested and cruelly martyred. For this, one hundred worshippers were taken, at St. Giles, in the very act of worship, and all of them put to cruel death. For this, Sir John Oldcastle, than whom a grander hero England never knew, was arrested, condemned, his property confiscated, his family made paupers, and himself, amid reproaches and insults, dragged to the Tyburn, where he was hung over a slow fire till he died. Still this hero never wavered. When the last spark of life was expiring, he warned the people to cling to the Bible, and with the words, "I die in triumph," his soul went to glory, leaving his dying words an ever enduring monument. "He was an Anabaptist, and deserved to die as a traitor," was the plaster which they put on the sore, the crime of his death made on their conscience. Still fearing, however, "lest these cursed Anabaptists" should continue to spread their heretical opinions, Parliament was induced to pass, among other measures for the suppression of heresy, the following:—"Whosoever shall read the Scriptures in English shall forfeit lands, chattels, goods and life, and be condemned as heretics. They shall be hanged for treason against the king, and then burned for heresy against God." Ah, me! it seems strange to us, who live under the stars and stripes of this glorious land, that such things could be; but we must remember, that was half a thousand years ago.

JOHN WICKLIFFE.

This Baptist reformer was born at Yorkshire

in 1324. He was educated at Oxford University and took clerical orders. Brought under the convicting power of the Holy Spirit, he struggled through the darkness and came into the light of God's pardoning love. Going direct to the Bible, he studied out a system of theology, which made him, in doctrine and practice, a Baptist. He believed the Bible to be the only law in matters of religion. He believed the church to be a company of converted men and women. He believed that the state has no power, inherent, to control man's religious belief. He believed that baptism was an outward sign of inward grace, and should be administered to none, except such as profess faith in Christ. All this goes to prove John Wickliffe a Baptist.

On comparing his views with those of the Lollards, Wickliffe found them to agree in all essential particulars, and henceforward the Lollards and the Wickliffites may be traced as one people; traced, yea, even by the light of the martyr fires that consumed them, till the day when the act of toleration, "England's Magna charta" gave them liberty to worship God.

Wickliffe was providentially preserved, and permitted to die a natural death; but forty years later, his bones were taken from their grave, and burned, and their ashes scattered to the four winds. He fell, but as the banner of truth fell from his nerveless grasp, it was seized by that intrepid reformer, John Huss, and carried into Bohemia, where it waved until the dawn of reformation broke upon the darkness of Europe.

Thus have we traced the footprints of Baptist principles, from the time and place where and whence they were first proclaimed to man, in that city of Zion, by Christ and his Apostles, in accordance with the Divine prediction given by Isaiah. Guided, often by the light of martyr fires, we have traced them through the Novatians in Italy, and the Donatists in Africa. We have seen those early christians persecuted, trodden under foot, and scattered, but carrying the seed of the gospel, only to plant it, wherever God should plant them. We have traced the same principles through the Paulicians and Bogomiles, into Armenia, where we found more than a hundred thousand martyr graves, containing the martyr dead of our brethren. From there we followed them to Thrace, from which we saw the light of a holy faith dawn on the waiting inhabitants of Bulgaria. We have traced them from there to Spain and France, and the secluded valleys that "lie peacefully at the base of the Alps, like an infant sleeping at its mother's feet." We have looked upon the red glare of the torch of death, as it waved its signal of destruction, and have seen the thousands of martyred slain, as they fell before the enemies of Christ and his church. We have turned from the bloody pathways of France and Spain, and followed the same footprints to Germany and Holland, the same reproachful name still clinging to their professors. Then turning our steps to Britain, we have seen the same altar fires lighted there, and ere long, also, the red glare of the burning faggots, piled to burn up heresy has shone out from that sea-girt isle. We have followed those faithful ones to the mountain fastnesses of Wales, where, deep in those retreats of safety, they kept the ordinances as Christ gave them, until reformation's morning broke over that fair island, when, like those on the continent, they came forth to welcome the coming morn, and hail the day star at its rising. We have seen the same disappointment, as with saddened hearts, they turned again to their hiding places, to patiently wait until the Lord himself should raise the means by which they should obtain rest from their enemies round about.

We have seen those people of one heart and one mind, the same in doctrinal belief, crossing and recrossing, mingling and intermingling, always holding fast to the same Bible truths, prophesying in sack cloth, "cast down but not destroyed," until, in God's good time, the 1260 years was fulfilled, when alike to one and the other, the days of their sack cloth were ended.

CHAPTER X.

WHAT OF THE NIGHT?

"Watchman, what of the night?"

We have now traced the footprints of Baptist principles through two separate lines of travel, from the days of the Apostles till the reformation. With them both we have found the beginning and the ending of the twelve hundred and sixty years of their prophesying in sack cloth.

We will now turn, once more, to the book of Revelation, and read the first three verses of the thirteenth chapter. Notice that this follows immediately after the measuring of the temple, the flight of the woman, and during the twelve hundred and sixty years, the witnesses were prophesying in sack cloth.

What is the interpretation? The beast which John saw rising out of the sea was the persecuting spirit. It developed among the people, indicated by "the sea." The "seven heads and ten horns," indicates the time and place of its first development. The seven-hilled city, in the days of the Roman Kings. The dragon represents the temporal power, from whom the persecuting power receives its authority to persecute. "It had the feet of a bear, and the mouth of a lion;" the former symbolizing the Greek, and the latter the Roman hierarchies. "The beast received a deadly wound, but the deadly wound was healed." This was fulfilled in the days of Cromwell and Charles II. Cromwell dissolved the long parliament with his sword, and largely secured liberty of conscience, not only in England, but in much of Europe besides. On the day when the treaty of alliance was to be signed between England and France, news came of a terrific massacre in Piedmont. On learning this, Cromwell refused to sign the treaty till it contained a clause insuring religious liberty to that people; declaring that he was not only "protector of England, but of protestantism in Europe." He wrote to several of the kings, pleading for religious liberty for their subjects, and went so far as to intimate, that if not otherwise granted, he would enforce it with the sword.

"But the deadly wound was healed." When about to see the realization of his hopes in securing liberty of conscience in all Europe, Cromwell "fell at the stroke of death." That licentious renegade and Catholic Charles II, was recalled to England and assumed the reins of government, with what result the student of history knows. The fires were rekindled, and the persecuting spirit again prevailed.

Go back a hundred years. A star had risen over Germany, a light had shown from Wittenburg. Luther had nailed his thesis to the door of his church, and thrown the gauntlet at Rome's very feet. His voice had reached the waiting thousands of God's suffering saints, and they came pouring forth from their secret places where they had worshipped God, in the hope that Luther would accept their sympathy and aid, and the reformation be made complete. Had Luther and his co-reformers but gone one step farther—had they but placed liberty of conscience by the side of justification by faith, the result would have been to lift the dark pall of religious persecution from the whole of Europe —Luther would have been a hundred times the hero he was, the fires of Smithfield would not have been relighted, and the world would be an hundred fold better for it today. But alas, for Luther! Great as he was, and grand as was his work, he missed the golden opportunity of the world's history. Alas, for those suffering, persecuted Baptists! Luther soon gave them to understand that justification by faith was one thing, and liberty of conscience was another. Saddened, disappointed, broken-hearted, they returned to their homes in the mountains and valleys, to await till the persecuting monster should be slain. They had gone to Erasmus with their sympathy, but he had scorned them because their were Anabaptists. Even the gentle spirited Melancthon gave them neither sympathy nor hope.

Let this fact be stated, in such bold characters that he that runs may read it. The reformation did not give, even in Germany, freedom to worship God. It was not till the war in the Netherlands, and the establishment of the

Dutch Republic that the persecuting power of Rome was broken on the continent, and not till the crowning of William and Mary, and the battle of the Boyne, that it was broken in Great Britain; the latter more than a century after the light of the reformation had first dawned on Europe.

We now come to what, at present, especially to southern Baptists, is the most important period of our history. It is that covered by what is known as the "Whitsitt controversy." This little book is not intended, either as a Baptist history, or as an answer to Dr. Whitsitt; the purpose being simply to trace a line of doctrinal principles. At the same time the reader will, no doubt, expect some notice to be taken of this question, and will feel a sense of disappointment if it is ignored. This is my only reason for trying to clear away, so far as I can, the doubt and uncertainty that hangs over this period.

I have not the pleasure of a personal acquaintance of Dr. Whitsitt, but from all I have learned, I conclude that the manliness of his character, the sweetness of his christian spirit, the fervor of his piety, the honesty of his motive and purpose, in all his life work, hitherto manifested, should preclude any charge of dishonesty, or deliberate unfaithfulness to his high trust. I believe he has made a mistake, but I am glad to believe it to be a mistake of the head and not of the heart. *

I think the mistake was two-fold. First—

---

* This was written before Bro. W. stated the same in the Baptist Reflector.

he is mistaken in the conclusion which he has drawn from the facts stated. Second—In the method he adopted of putting his conclusion before the public. I think I can appreciate the thought that prompted the action. He honestly believed his conclusion to be correct, and, believing this, he saw no reason why everybody should not be made acquainted with it. He overlooked, however, this fact. There is a wide difference between a conclusion or inference drawn from a set of facts, and an estab- but until it is plainly established, beyond the lished truth. The inference may be correct; power of denial, it is only an inference, and not an established truth. In view of the fact that his inference was in direct opposition to the established belief of his denomination for two hundred years, it was unfortunate that he did not first make known his inference to the denomination, of which he was a loved and trusted member, and let it first become an established truth, before giving it to the world.

The Baptists cannot be blamed for being sensitive on any question involving their allegiance to Christ, or the stability of their ordinances; and they are quick to challenge any statement, from whatever sorce, that throws any doubt on the Scriptural validity of their baptism. For nearly nineteen centuries this has been their attitude, and from it they have never swerved, even though it has led hundreds of thousands of them to prison and to death. Surely, they cannot be expected to surrender it now, without proof of their mistake, that will not admit of a doubt. All this I write with the most kindly feeling, as ready to accord to Dr. Whitsitt honesty of intention, as I am firm in my belief that he was mistaken.

The careful reader of these pages will, doubtless, have discovered, what it may be unnecessary to repeat, that it makes not the slightest difference with our ability to trace an unbroken line of Baptist principles from the Apostles down, whether Dr. Whitsitt's inference be correct, or incorrect. I have already shown that by two distinct lines, we are able to trace our principles to England, viz:—Through the Voidois, Albigenses and Waldenses; and also through the Dutch Baptists of Holland.

The fire carried to England, by Lollard, and fanned into a mighty flame by his followers and the Wickliffites never became fully extinguished. They were, without doubt, still in England, when, in 1633, the brethren referred to in the "Kiffin Manuscript" sent to Holland and received baptism from the Dutch Mennonite Baptists. It is, however, through these latter that we trace our American Baptists, in their line of descent.

Let us now study this period a little more carefully, and see if the facts justify Dr. Whitsitt's conclusion, that immersion had become extinct in England previous to 1641. Certainly, if immersion had become extinct, Baptists had also; for to talk of Baptists who do not immerse, is the height of absurdity. I think it can be shown that neither the one nor the other had become extinct.

Had Dr. Whitsitt said that Pedo-Baptist adult immersion had become extinct at that date, he would have been correct; but had he said that Pedobaptist immersion had become extinct, even then he would have been incorrect. If it be claimed that Dr. Whitsitt's statement disproves the fact of Scriptural immersion, at least in England, at the period mentioned, I answer with these two facts: First, by the testimony of the most learned Pedobaptists, who have made the most careful investigation, it is proved that immersion was the universal custom for fully thirteen centuries; and, Second, that in the sixteenth century, so general was the practice of immersion in England, that Elizabeth, first born child of Henry VIII, and Anna Bolynn, was publicly immersed, September 11th, 1533, or just one hundred years before those brethren referred to by Dr. Whitsitt, sent to Holland for it. Four years from the above date, Edward, the royal son, was carried to their church, and there publicly immersed also. If, then, immersion had become so lost in England that Baptists could not find it, how came it to be so popular, that even Pedobaptist royalty must needs observe it publicly in the immersion of the king's children? The truth is that, while in the English, as well as other reformed churches, believers' baptism, had been almost universally replaced by infant baptism, immersion was still the prevailing custom, in England; so much so, that, by a decree of Queen Elizabeth, fonts for the immersion of infants were put in all the prominent buildings of the English state church, and the priests were forbidden by law to perform baptism in any other way.

Henry VIII seceded from Rome, and became head of the church of England in 1534. This led many of the Baptists on the continent to hope for liberty of conscience in England, and go to that country. In this they were mistaken. A proclamation was issued against "Those strangers, born out of the land, who are come into this realm, who, albeit, they were baptised in infancy, they have, of their own presumption, been rebaptised;" and so numerous were these people that a creed was drawn up for them to sign. This creed differs in many particulars from the belief of the Baptists, except that the mode of baptism is not mentioned, a fact, proving conclusively, that immersion had not yet come to be disputed.

In 1539 milder measures were resorted to by Henry, and as a result, great numbers of Baptists, from various parts of the continent took refuge in England, and at once began active missionary operations. Of these people— Fuller, the historian, declared, "They are but the Donatists new dipped;" proving not only that they immersed, but that they held to the ancient Baptist faith.

In 1547 Henry died, leaving Edward VI,

then only nine years old at the head of the government. His advisors being more liberal in their views, milder measures prevailed, "Persecution ceased, prison doors were thrown open, and many refugees returned." Others came from other parts, so that by 1554, the Baptists had become so numerous, it was found necessary to resort to severer measures for their suppression. A commission was therefore instituted, with instructions to hunt out all Baptists, and if they refused to renounce their Baptist faith, they were to be given over to the secular power to be punished. It was admitted that they were good, honest citizens, and pure christians, and that there lives were without reproach, but their crime was that of standing by the teaching of Christ, in spite of the requirement of the king.

Edward died July 6th, and on October 1st, of the same year, Mary was crowned. Her first act was to restore, so far as possible, the power and authority of the Pope. Her second, to institute a bitter and cruel persecution against the Lollards. She appointed a royal commission to hunt them out, destroy their conventicles, burn their printing presses, and do all possible to prevent the spread of their doctrines.

Fortunately, she was only permitted to reign five years, but in that period she wrote her history in blood. No less than 277 martyrs

were cruelly put to death by her orders, or
more than an average of one every week, for
her entire reign.

On the death of Mary, Elizabeth was
crowned, and many fancied that the reign of
persecution was over. She at once issued a
proclamation, inviting all who had been banished on account of religion to return. Very
many accepted the invitation, both Baptists
and other dissenters, who had fled to Geneva,
Switzerland, and had there learned the practice of sprinkling, which, by that time had
become quite common among the Swiss,
although it had not yet obtained a foothold in
England. On returning, they introduced it in
England, but these were not Baptists, but persons who had imbibed the doctrines of Calvin. So far from immersion being extinct
in England at that date, this is the first
authenticated mention of any other mode; and
it was at once forbidden by the queen and the
bishops, and a decree issued that nothing but
immersion would be practiced, unless in case
of extreme weakness, when it would suffice to
pour water on the child.

The truth is, the constant changes of attitude on the part of the rulers towards the Baptists—now tolerating them, now persecuting
them, only to return to toleration again, long
enough to inspire hope, then again enacting cruel and oppressive measures, so saddened and dis-
heartened the Baptists, as to preclude any very
active measures for the spread of their prin-

ciples. Add to this the fact, that Elizabeth, during her reign, issued against them no less than three decrees of banishment, and that those repressive measures were vigorously enforced by Elizabeth's two successors, and it is not to be wondered at, if Baptists and immersion do not stand out very prominently during this period of England's history. There were plenty of Baptists, and plenty of immersion there; but, as their bitter enemy, Dr. Featley puts it, "By the diligence of the magistrates, and the ecclesiastics, they were kept covered" —that is, suppressed, so that they, of course, do not prominently stand out during that period.

Parliament had made Henry the head of the church. Mary had made the pope head, when Henry died, and Elizabeth made herself the head, and all, like Saul the Pharisee, honestly believed they were doing God's service, when they were persecuting the Baptists.

"As a result of the tyranical spirit of Luther, in Germany," says Mosheim, "schools of German Baptists had passed into Holland and the Netherlands, where they had propagated their sentiments in various places." A great many of these passed into England, and began missionary operations there, with great success. This was too much for the queen and bishops, and a decree was issued requiring all Baptists to leave the realm within twenty-one days. This was in 1560; and in 1593 a still

more severe decree was issued, commanding all
Anabaptists, and other heretics, whether for-
eigners or natives, to leave the realm under
severest penalties.   By this time the war in
the Netherlands, had resulted in the establishment of the Dutch republic, with libert·· of conscience as one of its basic principles; and
many Baptists took refuge there, resulting in
opening a still wider channel of communication between the Baptists of the two countries.
No doubt many remained in England, prefer-
ring to worship God in secret than to suffer
banishment, hopin·· and waiting for God to
come to their deliverance in his own good time.
But even then, Baptists were not, by any
means, extinct in England.   This is proved by
the hosts of them that came out into the light,
when the ban was again lifted.

This was the condition of things at the opening of the sixteenth century.   In 1602 Elizabeth closed her reign, and was succeeded by
James the Second, and he by Charles the First.
The repressive measures of Elizabeth were not
quite so vigorously enforced by James the
Second, and still further lightened by his suc-
cessor.   As a consequence Baptists not only
retained their hold in England, but soon began
to increase; so much so that in 1611 we find
the Baptists who had returned from Holland
publishing a confession of faith containing
twenty-seven articles, representing the views
of the General Baptists.   It should be stated

here that by this time the Baptists of England had become recognized as "General" and "Particular" Baptists; the former holding to the doctrine of the general atonement, the latter to the Calvanistic view, or particular atonement. About this period Edward Wightman was condemned and burned for holding to the doctrine of the Dutch Baptists. In 1615 the Baptists published a small book condemning persecution, and subscribing themselves as "Christ's unworthy witnesses, commonly but falsely called Anabaptists." In 1620 they sent an earnest petition to the king and parliament, in which they refer to having "suffered imprisonment for many years in divers counties of England."

This brings us down to 1633, the time when the church referred to by Dr. Whitsett, sent to Holland "to secure the ancient rite of immersion." This church was composed of fifty-three members who had, in a body, separated themselves from the Independents, or Brownists, and decided to organize themselves into a Baptist church. In order to be certain of securing their immersion from the line of the "ancient Baptists," as they termed them, they sent their pastor to Holland to be immersed there; and he, on his return, immersed the rest, thus securing through the Holland Baptists their immersion in a direct line from the Apostles.

Now, so far from condemning those brethren for their action, I think it highly commend-

able; but does it prove that either Baptists
or immersion had become extinct at that time?
Most certainly not. Neither the document referred to by Dr. Whitsitt—the "Kiffin manuscript," nor the facts as they existed, warrants
any such conclusion. All the document states
is that "So far as these brethren knew there
were none whose immersion would be satisfactory to them; not being certain whether
they had retained the ancient rite or had begun it again." Dr. Whitsitt's opinion that
"the reason for sending to Holland was because immersion had become extinct in England," is not only unsupported but is at variance with the facts.

Holland had given liberty of conscience in
1679, or one hundred and eleven years before
it obtained in England. During all the time
from 1579 to 1640 there had been a constant
coming and going between the Baptists of the
two countries; Holland being the refuge of the
English Baptists whenever banished from their
own country. There were thus a thousand
chances for the Baptists of England to connect
themselves with the ancient baptism of the
Dutch, or Mennonite Baptists. Where then
was the difficulty? Simply here. Those brethren, coming out, as they did, from the Brownists, were entirely unacquainted with the Baptists of England. They knew of the decrees of
banishment against them. They knew of the
laws for their suppression. They knew how
they had been kept "covered," as their enemies

boasted, and their worship, their baptisms, a
their very names having to be kept secret.
There were plenty of Baptists, and plenty of
immersion in England, only those brethren
did not have sufficient knowledge of them to be
certain whether they had retained the ancient
form or been compelled to begin it again after
the ban was lifted. The fact that they knew
so much about the Holland Baptists and their
immersion is explained by the other fact that
in Holland the Baptists had already had religious liberty for half a century. That is all
there is in the Kiffin manuscript, and the fact
therein related about which so much has been
said and written.

If well attested facts are any evidence that
neither Baptists nor immersion was extinct in
England during the period referred to, it is as
fully proven, as that there are Baptists today
in Tennessee. This is proven by the following facts, additional to those already given.
In 1536, complaint was made that certain persons, who had been baptised in their infancy,
had renounced their former baptism, and been
rebaptized. In 1533, the Baptists "did very
much to pester the church, and openly dispute
in public places." In 1547, Henry VIII died,
having put to death, by his orders or permis-
sion, 72,000 persons. These were not his own
people. Who were they?

In 1549, complaint was made that Baptists
were in many parts of England, one man report-

ing that he knew of five hundred in one town.
In 1573, a meeting being held by a church of
the Dutch Baptists ,at Aldergate, in London,
was broken up, and twenty-seven of the worshipers were committed to prison, and, afterwards, some of them were burned at Smithfield.   In 1583, a very large church of Dutch
Baptists was known to exist at Norwich.   In
1618, there was published in England a little
book entitled "A Treatise on Baptism."   It was
translated from the Dutch language.   In 1620
the Baptists came out openly and made an appeal, setting forth their reasons for leaving the
established church.   In 1641 a meeting was
held in Southwark, in which eighty Baptists
passed a resolution that the magistrate was
only to be obeyed in civil matters.   In 1641,
one Barber published a small book against infant baptism,for which he was imprisoned for 11
months.   In 1642 very bitter complaint was
made that the Baptists were dipping hundreds
of people over head and ears.   By this time
there were seven Baptist churches in London,
and forty-seven in the country.   It is surely
unnecessary to pursue the subect further, to
convince the reader that Dr. Whitsitt is mistaken in his conclusion that immersion was
extinct in England in 1641.

I have not had the opportunity of reading
the Doctor's article in Johnson's Encyclopedia,
nor the St. George pamphlets to which he
refers, and have therefore confined myself to

such statements as I have read from his own pen. But, if on investigation, the St. George pamphlets afford no more positive proof than the Doctor in his position, than that which I have so far seen, Baptists need not in the least worry over the result. Indeed, I confidently predict that in the end this matter will very greatly result in benefit to our denomination.

We will next trace our principles across the Atlantic, and see them planted in the New World.

CHAPTER XI.

"AN ARMY WITH BANNERS."
"In the name of our God we will set up our banners."

To trace the history of the rise and progress of Baptist principles in America would require many volumes. All I propose here is to give an authentic statement of their first planting, some account of their early trials, and close with a few facts and figures, indicating their present standing and influence as a denomination.

I have stated in a former chapter that the Baptists of this country do not owe their origin to Roger Williams. Neither he nor the church he organized has any connection with American Baptist history, except that it was organized, existed four months, and then dissolved, without leaving anything to perpetuate the work it had done. We must look elsewhere for the beginning of our people in this country.

When the Puritans embarked on board the Mayflower, and turned her prow toward the New World, "What sought they? Freedom to worship God." But they overlooked—or, perhaps it were better to say, they had not yet come to apprehend one great fact. That is, that liberty of conscience can never exist, in common with the right of the state to control a man in his doctrine and worship. Establish either one and you are bound to destroy the other. This was the mistake of Luther; this was the mistake of the Pilgrim Fathers.

It is not, therefore, to be wondered at, if we find that the history of the early Baptists of America follows that of their forefathers and marks a pathway of fire. Baptists have known what religious persecution was even in free America. Fines and imprisonments were common in the early days as well as acts for the suppression of the Anabaptists passed by the Colonial Legislatures. One of the most sublime scenes ever enacted on the American continent was enacted in Virginia at the trial of Lewis Craig, Joseph Craig and Aaron Bledsoe for the crime of preaching the gospel of the Son of God. The Court had assembled. The judge was in his seat; the prisoners at the bar and the clerk reading the indictment, when Patrick Henry entered, having ridden on horseback sixty miles to volunteer his services in defense of the prisoners. After the King's attorney had presented the case, Patrick Henry arose, and taking the indictment, he said: "May it please the court, I think I heard this paper read by the prosecutor as I entered this court. Did I hear it distinctly, or was it a mistake of my own? If I heard rightly, these men are about to be tried for a crime. What is that crime?" Pausing a moment, he repeated it—slowly and in most solemn tones, "For preaching the gospel of the Son of God."

Pausing again, he waved the paper three times around his head, and lifting his hands and eyes toward heaven, he cried out, "Great God!" Then in a speech that, for deep pathos, burning eloquence and convincing power has never been excelled, he laid down the principles of soul-freedom. The judge looked solemn, the clerk looked pale, and the King's attorney shook like an aspen, and the assembly was being worked up to a point beyond self control, when the judge ended the scene by shouting, "Sheriff, discharge those men." This was in Virginia, where a hundred years previous, a law had been passed, imposing a fine of two hundred pounds of tobacco upon any person who should refuse to carry his child to the parson for baptism.

In New England the Baptists fared no better. The statutes enacted, and the testimony of early writers prove conclusively that there were Baptists in New England some time before Roger Williams founded his Rhode Island Colony. As early as 1643, or only twenty-three years after the Puritans had landed at Plymouth, we find a colonial enactment for the suppression of "the Anabaptists." This act recites that those Anabaptists had appeared among them "Since their coming to New England;" and Cotton Mather speaks of some "Godly Anabaptists who had been with them"—the Puritans—"from the beginning."

The first Baptist churches that I have been

able to find, whose history can be traced, are two; both organized in 1638. One by Hanserd Knollys, and the other by John Clark, and in 1639 six men were arrested for organizing a Baptist church at Weymouth, fourteen miles south of Boston. Knollys and Clark came to America from England, the former remaining but three years, so that but little is known of the church which he founded. The church founded by John Clark, it is claimed, has had an unbroken existence from that period until now, so that the old Baptist church at Newport can proudly say, and with good reason, "I am the mother of you all."

There is some question, however, whether this church was organized in 1638 or 1639. Two facts I think are sufficient to settle this question. The first is, that in the minutes of the Philadelphia Association, there is a record still preserved, stating that John Callender, in 1738 preached the one hundredth anniversary sermon of the organization of the First Baptist Church of Rhode Island. The second is, that the monument erected to the memory of John Clark contains an inscription which recites that Clark came to Newport in March, 1638, and that shortly after viz. the 24th of the same month, obtained a deed of land from the Indians, and shortly after that gathered a church and became its pastor. From all the evidences I have thus been able to consult, I think it may be safely affirmed that the first

Baptist church of America, whose history we can now trace, was organized by John Clark and his associates, at Newport, Rhode Island, in 1638. Other churches went out from this, but the progress was slow for several years, owing to the severe repressive measures, to prevent the spread of Baptist principles. Other Baptists in time came in, from both Holland and England, so that the American Baptists can rightly claim their descent from the Baptists of England and Holland, and through them trace an unbroken line of principles, back through those ancient bodies, whose brief history I have here given, directly to the churches founded by Christ and his Apostles.

A single reference to a few figures, showing the growth of our denomination and its present strength, and our task will be finished.

The Baptist year book for 1895, published by the American Baptist Publication Society, which by the way, is a most valuable book, and should be in every Baptist family, gives us the following figures, which should be studied with deep interest, and call for devout gratitude.

In the United States we have the following:

Associations, 1,551; ministers, 27,774; churches 40,064; baptised last year, 176,058; total membership, 3,720,235. Children in Sunday schools, 1,779,886. Money raised for all denominational purposes, $11,755,118. The present membership of our Baptist churches is about equal to the entire population of the colonies at the declaration of independence.

In educational institutions, we have seven theological seminaries, with sixty-seven instructors, 1002 pupils, 990 preparing for the ministry. Value of their property is $3,774,850. These seminaries have endowments amounting to $2,665,091.

In universities and colleges, we have—Institutions, 37; teachers, 807; endowment, $13,238,549. Value of property, $22,722,163. In female seminaries, 29 institutions; 370 professors, 3,824 pupils; $1,248,885 endowment, and property valued at $4,063,297.

Of other schools for both sexes, or males only, we have: 64 institutions, 530 professors, 14,341 students; value of endowment $1,344,700. Value of property, $4,167,730. For the education of negroes and Indians, we have: institutions, 33; teachers, 293. Endowments, $117,500. Value of property, $1,398,830. This gives us a grand total of 169 institutions of learning, with 2,067 professors; 36,016 students. Value of endowment, $18,614, 695, and value of school property, $36, 126, 870.

The Baptists of the world number: churches, 46,520, with a total membership of 4,447,074.

During the year 1895, the Baptists of the United States raised for religious purposes $11,755,118, of which $1,172,909 was for missions.

Surely, the little one has become a thousand, and the small one a strong nation. To God be all the glory.

APPENDIX.

Much of the material incorporated in the body of this little pamphlet has lain by me for some years. Years ago I became an enthusiastic student of Baptist History, and have diligently continued it, with such sources of information as I could, in my limited way, secure. Besides such secular histories as would aid me, notably, Gibbon's, I have read the church histories of Mosheim, Neander, Waddington, Jones and Schaff. Of Baptist Histories, Benedict, Armitage, Cramp, W. R. Williams, Orchard, "Foreign" and "English" Baptists, and most of the smaller works that have come in my way. I have consulted and compared the articles bearing on the subject in most of the cyclopaedias, and, in fact, sought such information, from any source possible, as I thought would aid me, in arriving at the truth concerning the people whose history I have so much delighted to study.

As I intended the book for popular reading, in the hands of the masses, I have thought it best to take the facts and ideas of the various authors consulted, and clothe them in my own language, rather than to give literal quotations, with name and page of author. Where literal quotations are given they are properly indicated. It has been, withal, my earnest desire to have the facts stated historically correct.

Up to the time of what is now known as the "Whitsitt Controversy," I had no doubt whatever of the perfect reliability of the various authors I had studied, although, in some minor particulars, they somewhat differed from one another.

It was not until my pamphlet was in the hands of my publishers, that I learned that our esteemed brother, Rev. Dr. Whitsitt, was preparing, and would soon publish, a book that would, undoubtedly, throw much new light on this whole subject. On learning this, I resolved, at once, to hold my own book back until I could secure his, and give it a most careful reading; and if, after reading his book, it should seem necessary, I would either re-write mine, or cancel the order for publication, even though I had paid for it mostly in advance. However, after giving Brother Whitsitt's book two most careful readings, I can find in it no reason why my own should not be given to the public—more especially as it lays no claim to being more than a simple effort to trace Baptist principles, rather than to give a history of the Baptist denomination.

In this connection I want to add a few words with reference to the reliabilty of those authors I have studied; especially "Orchard's History of the English Baptists." I believed those authors to be fairly reliable, and I am glad to be able to write that, so far, I have found no cause to change my opinion. While Dr. Whitsitt did not intend to write of the early Baptists, his brief references thereto do not, in any way, conflict with what has heretofore been written.

I am aware that some doubt has been suggested as to the reliability of "Orchard's History." The author of that work has gone to his reward, and is no longer here to answer for himself. It seems meet, therefore, that I should add a few words in his defense.

I have never read any suggestion of doubt as to his honesty, either of motive or methods. This fact admitted, what are the other facts? Dr. Orchard was born, lived and died in the very land where all these historical events occurred. I refer now to the English Baptists. If our American authors spent "several months" studying historical data in England, Dr. Orchard spent thirty years in the same study. If they had ready access to the British Museum, the Bodlein Library, and other valuable sources of information, Orchard not only had the same, but he availed himself of it to the fullest extent. There is no source of information open to them that was not open to him; and none of which he did not, so far as I can learn, avail himself, unless it was the testimony furnished by Professor Scheffer, of Amsterdam, and on which, truth compels me to say, I do not place as much reliance as does Brother Whitsitt, for reasons which I will intimate further on. Indeed, after carefully comparing Orchard's book with that of Dr. Whitsitt, I am more fully impressed than before with the reliability of the former. They quote, largely, the same authorities, give the same dates and state the same facts. The greatest difference is in the conclusion which they draw from the facts stated.

Now, as to Brother Whitsitt's book, I have no intention of giving a review of it, or of doing more than to give briefly the reasons why I cannot agree with the author, in the position he has taken, leaving to others of far greater ability to review the book, as they may feel it to be duty.

So far as I shall go, I shall try to write honestly and fearlessly, seeking only to satisfy my own judgment and conscience, regardless of how much others may agree with, or differ from me.

As to the controversy that has grown out of the "Whitsitt Matter," I am convinced that Dr. Whitsitt has been seriously misunderstood, and, as a result, without intending it, much misrepresented. Indeed, "A Tempest in a Teapot," on a large scale, will best express the idea I have regarding this great controversy. So far as the book is concerned, there is nothing in it to invalidate the Doctor's claim to being a Sound Baptist. The whole issue is narrowed down to this single question. Did, or did not believer's immersion become extinct in England, for a longer or shorter period prior to 1641? So far as affecting Baptist descent

goes, what does it matter whether it did or did
not? It is admitted that Baptists existed elsewhere, and that believers' immersion was practiced by John, commanded by Christ, and has
continued from the Apostolic age till now.
Here is the bold declaration of Dr. Whitsitt in
the very first paragraph of his introduction:
"Immersion, as a religious rite, was practiced
by John the Baptist about the year 30, of our
era, and was solemnly enjoined by our Saviour
on all His ministers till the end of time. No
other observance was in use for baptism in
New Testament times. The practice, though
sometimes greatly perverted, has yet been continued from the Apostolic age down to our
own. As I understand the Scriptures, immersion is essential to Christian baptism."

This settles the question as to the soundness
of Dr. Whitsitt's views on believers' baptism.
Hereafter, while the above declaration stands,
let no one quote Dr. Whitsitt as authority for
the statement that "Immersion as a Christian
ordinance was unknown prior to 1641." He has
made no such statement as that, and hereafter
to repeat it will be willful and wicked misrep-
resentation.

This being true, Baptists could admit all
that Dr. Whitsitt claims, without, in the least,
weakening their claim to Apostolic antiquity,
or losening a single stone in the solid foundation on which their New Testament practice
rests. Suppose, if such a thing could be, that
a hundred years from now, some one, in writ-

ing a history of American Baptists, should make the discovery that, from 1750 to 1850, there was not a Baptist, nor a believers' immersion in the state of Tennessee—what difference would that make with our American Baptist history, beyond the fact, that, while all the rest of the United States had thousands of Baptists, Tennessee was, for a hundred years, without the blessing of the New Testament practice? So in this case. The question is not whether there still existed believers' baptism, in the manner required by Scripture, but whether in that little piece of territory called England it existed during the short period referred to.

I am convined that if Dr. Whitsitt's claim, with proper explanation, had been admitted by all, it would have done our denomination far less injury than the unfortunate controversy that has grown out of the matter. All this, however, only in the interest of truth, without in the least impugning the motives or action of those brethren, who, like myself, as honestly believe Dr. Whitsitt to be wrong, as he believes himself to be right.

Concerning the Doctor's position, and the evidence he has produced to establish it, I believe every unprejudiced reader will cheerfully grant him this much:

1. That he honestly believes the position he has taken to be correct; and that he is so convinced by the testimony he has furnished.

2. That he honestly believes the testimony sufficient to convince anyone else who is not

wedded to a preconceived opinion to the contrary. That he honestly believes all this, no man who reads his book without prejudice can doubt. This much in justice to Brother Whitsitt.

And yet, as honestly desiring to have the truth, as Brother Whitsitt possibly can be, I am compelled to differ from him, and strongly dissent from the conclusion he draws from the testimony he has furnished. So far from being convinced—and I was certainly not prejudiced in my reading, for my sympathy was with Brother Whitsitt—after giving his book two most careful readings, studying it the last time, paragraph by paragraph, I find myself differing from him more strongly than before

I am conscious that this is a strong statement—nay almost presumptious—to be made by a humble preacher, touching the position of one so learned, so well read, and, in every way so much my superior as Dr. Whitsitt; but I have very much misread the kind disposition and liberal spirit of our brother if he does not cheerfully concede to the humblest of his brethren the same privilege of free thought and free speech that he asks for himself.

Having stated so frankly my disagreement with Brother Whitsitt, I am in duty bound to give, with reasonable plainness, the reasons for such disagreement.

It should be borne in mind here, that all men are not impressed in the same way by the same facts. It takes more to convince some men than it does others, of the truth of a given statement. I have no doubt that some who have withheld their decision till they have read Brother Whitsitt's book, are now fully convinced that he has made out his case; while others, equally honest, will, I doubt not, be as fully convinced that he has failed to maintain the claim he so confidently put forward.

It would be presumption on my part, and prove me guilty of self-conceit, were I to pretend to be as well posted in these historical matters as my brother is, and so, in giving my reasons for differing from him, I shall confine myself exclusively to his book, entirely ignoring all evidence elsewhere found.

The issue, as I understand it, is this: Dr. Whitsitt affirms that prior to 1641, believers' immersion had become utterly extinct in England; and the purpose of his book is to give the evidence to prove it. The question then is, does the evidence he has given prove his statement true, beyond a reasonable doubt? This is what he is bound to do, to maintain the position he has taken.

It is a universal rule in evidence, that a thing or fact, once existing, is assumed to continue to exist, unless there is positive proof that it has ceased to exist. In such a case, circumstantial evidence is not admissable. The proof must be clear, positive and convincing, establishing the fact beyond the possibility of a reasonable doubt.

In applying this rule to the issue under consideration, let us, first, inquire whether immersion did exist in England prior to 1641, and if there is a reasonable probability of its having continued; and second, notice the testimony on which Dr. Whitsitt relies to establish the fact of its extinction.

On page 23, we are told that "In earliest times immersion prevailed in England as elsewhere," and on page 33, it is shown that it was continued longer in England than on the continent, or anywhere else. Here, then, we have the fact of its existence clearly established; all that is required now is to show a reasonable probability that it continued to exist.

On page 29, we have the following quotation from Dr. Wall: "The offices and litergies for public baptism in the church of England did, all along, so far as I can learn, enjoin dipping, without any mention of sprinkling or pouring." The Doctor adds, that the book of common prayer for 1549 required trine immersion, but allowed, if the child were weak, it would suffice to pour water upon it. In 1552, a new prayer book appeared enjoining a single immersion, and making pouring optional in case of weakness. On page 30, we are told that in 1571, immersion was practiced by royal decree, and church wardens were required to furnish facilities for the purpose. This was still further decreed in 1584.

This, then, is the position and practice of the Church of England, under royal requirement, as late as 1584—or only fifty-seven years be-

fore we find the Baptists of England openly
practicing the same form of baptism, while, so
far as we can learn, the only influence acting
against it, is that of the Presbyterian refugees
recently returned from Switzerland. Will any
reasonable man suppose that the persecutions
of those re-baptising would be any more severe,
where it was done in the prescribed form, than
when done in violation of royal decree? Such
a conclusion is absurd. The persecution of the
Baptists in those days was not because of their
form of baptism, but because they refused to
recognize the authority of the state church.
When, therefore, they immersed, they performed the act required by royal decree;
when they sprinkled or poured they not only
went against the state church, but violated
the royal decree as well. The argument from
persecution is, therefore, all in favor of immersion instead of any other mode, up to at least
1584.

Let us now go on to 1644, and, putting our
stakes down there, run our line back to a meeting place. On pages 70 to 72 we have an effort,
on the part of the Doctor, to prove Dr. Armitage mistaken, when he states, on the authority of Dr. Featley's "Dippers Dipt," that Baptists had been practicing immersion for twenty
years previous to 1644. It is no wonder that
Dr. Whitsitt makes a strong effort to prove
Dr. Armitage mistaken, for if his statement is
allowed to stand, it upsets the Doctor's position by seventeen years. I think, however,

that I will be able to convince every unprejudiced reader that it is Dr. Whitsitt, not Dr. Armitage, that is laboring under the mistake.

Dr. Armitage made his statement under the authority of Dr. Featley's book, entitled, "The Dippers Dipt; or the Anabaptist Plunged Head and Ears."

He gives the following quotation to show the manner of their baptism: "They flock in great multitudes to their Jordans and both sexes enter into the rivers and are dipt after their manner. * * * * And as they defile our rivers with their impure washings, and our pulpits with their false prophecies, and fanatical enthusiasms, so the presses groan and sweat under the load of their blasphemies." I pause here to remark, by way of parenthesis—the reader will notice that Dr. Featley uses the term "washings," when he means immersion; we will therefore be justified in understanding the same term in the same sense, where we meet it in other places. To proceed: Dr. Armitage gives a second quotation from another page, as follows: "This venomous serpent is the Ana-Baptist, who in these later times, first showed his shining head and speckled skin, and thrust out his sting, near the place of my residence, for more than twenty years ago." From these two quotations, Dr. Armitage very justly concludes that immersion was practiced near Dr. Featley's residence for more than twenty years previous to 1644, or seventeen years before Dr. Whitsitt now claims that it was introduced into

APPENDIX. 135

England. Dr. Whitsitt admits that both these
quotations refer to the same class of people,
but insists that they refer to different modes
of baptizing at different times. To prove Dr.
Armitage mistaken, and that it was sprinkling
those Anabaptists practiced, twenty years
before, he quotes the following, also from Dr.
Featley's book: "But of late, since the unhappy
distraction which our sins have brought upon
us, the temporal sword being otherwise employed, and the spiritual locked up fast in the
scabbord, this sect among others, hath so far
presumed upon the patience of the state, that
it hath held weekly conventicles, rebaptized
hundreds of men and women together in the twi-
light, in rivulets and some arms of the Thames
and elsewhere, dipping them over head and
ears." From this quotation, Dr. Whitsitt ar-
gues that the sect first sprang up twenty years
before, but that they had only recently begun
the practice of immersion. To this I answer:
Does Dr. Featley in the above quotation intend
to describe a new mode of baptism, or does he
emphasize the fact that, "since the sword has
been otherwise employed" those people have
become bolder and more open and frequent with
their baptism? Undoubtedly the latter. Unfortunately one part of Dr. Featley's statement has been left out, which will make the
whole clear. It is as follows: "This fire,
which under the reigns of Queen Elizabeth,
and King James, and our gracious Sovereign
till now, was covered in England under the

ashes; or if it break out at any time, by the care of the ecclesiastics and civil magistrates, it was soon put out. But of late, since the unhappy distractions which our sins have brought upon us," etc., as quoted by Dr. Whitsitt. There is not a line nor a hint here as to any new baptism, different from that which they had always practiced. In these several quotations Dr. Featley makes three distinct statements:

1. That this sect existed during the reign of Elizabeth and subsequent sovereigns, but by the power of the civil magistrates they were kept "covered"—that is, subdued and kept under.

2. That more than twenty years before, they had appeared with their dipping near his residence. Doubtless, they were again put down as usual.

3. That since the "unhappy distractions" referred to, they had become so bold that they held weekly meetings, and practiced their immersions wherever convenient, in the same manner as they had done twenty years ago.

I notice another unfortunate omission made by our brother which, when supplied, proves beyond a possible doubt not only that Brother Whitsitt, rather than Dr. Armitage is mistaken, but that Dr. Featley himself bears the most undoubted testimony that immersion had been practiced by some "ancient Anabaptists."

On page 73 the Doctor quotes from Dr. Featley's argument against the Baptist confession of faith, that prescribes—"dipping or plunging, as the way and manner of administering the ordinance of baptism." Touching that Brother Whitsitt quotes Featley as follows. "This article is wholly sowsed with the new leaven, of Anabaptism. I say new leaven for it cannot be proved that any of the ancient Anabaptists maintained any such position * * * It is not essential to baptism, neither do the texts in the margin conclude any such thing."

It will be seen that Dr. Whitsitt has done here just what he charges Dr. Armitage with having done. He quotes Dr. Featley's statement up to the word "position," leaves out the qualifying phrase, and putting his own construction on it, uses it as evidence that the Anabaptists had not practiced immersion. Had the whole quotation been given any reader would have seen that Dr. Featley does not claim that the ancient Anabaptists did not practice immersion, but, on the contrary bears the strongest testimony that they did. Following is the whole quotation, as given by Dr. Armitage. "It cannot be proved that any of the ancient Anabaptists maintained any such position, there being three ways of baptism; either by dipping, washing, or sprinkling." It will be clearly seen that the quotation complete conveys a very different meaning from that which Brother Whitsitt gives it. The "position" here referred to as held by the Baptists and which Dr. Featley was contending against was not that dipping

was the only Scriptural baptism. He says that
among the Anabaptists there were three modes
practiced,—"dipping, washing and sprinkling."

This is what every well informed Baptist admits; and what I had already stated in the body
of my book.

Dr. Featley could thus very truly declare
that Anabaptists and even "ancient Anabaptists," as he understood the term, did practice
"washing and sprinkling" for it was true;
but if these combined statements of Dr.
Featley do not convey the idea that those
particular Anabaptists of whom he writes, did
immerse, and that they had continued that
practice from the days of Queen Elizabeth—albeit they had been, for the most part, kept
"covered" by the civil power, then it is useless to employ words to convey ideas. I
stand with Dr. Armitage.

But I will make this position still stronger.
One page 68, Dr. Whitsitt makes the following
quotation, referring to three varieties of Anabaptists, who had gone from England to Amsterdam, and who were there in 1611. Doubtless this was because of one of the many
decrees of banishment. Of these three varieties of Anabaptists, it is asserted: "Master
Smyth, an Anabaptist of one sort, and Master
Hilwise of another, and Master Busher of another." Which sort does Master Busher represent? Let him speak for himself, as Dr.
Whitsitt quotes him on page 69. "And such
as shall willingly and gladly receive it (the

word) he hath commanded to be baptised in water, that is, dipped for dead in the water." Dr. Whitsitt admits the genuineness of this quotation, but seeks to break its force by asserting that we do not know enough about Fusher to decide whether he practiced immersion or not. That is, when a Christian author states that Christ requires immersion, we do not know whether he is an immersionist in practice. Admitting this, may not the English Baptists of a hundred years from now, question whether or not Dr. Whitsitt was an immersionist in practice? Undoubtedly Busher represented the immersing variety of Anabaptists.

This is the sect that Dr. Featley says was "kept covered" in England, until the unhappy "distractions," when they came out boldly, and openly practiced their immersions, very much to the disgust of good Doctor Featley.

And this view is still further strengthened by the declaration of Dr. Featley that there were other sects that had also "presumed on the patience of the state." He says: "This sect among others."—that is other sects. What other sects? Why the other sects of Anabaptists who also defied the state church, and went on preaching believers' baptism only, but poured their members instead of immersing them.

You see how this complaint of Dr. Featley that "this sect among others" is in perfect accord with the testimony furnished by Dr. Whitsitt that "there were three varieties of Anabaptists." Dr. Featley does not say they all immersed, but he does say that "This sect among others hath so far presumed on the patience of the state that it hath held weekly conventicles, baptised hundreds of men and women,"etc. Each sect "presumed on the patience of the state" to carry out its practices in its own way.

I have thus, from Dr. Whitsitt's own book, traced immersion back from where we planted our stakes in 1644 to Queen Elizabeth in 1558, or twenty-six years back of the time when immersion was the prevailing custom in the English church, and maintained by royal authority; that is, that believers' immersion overlaps that required by royal decree, and practiced in the English church, by twenty-six years.

It should be stated here, in justice to Brother Whitsitt, that he does not dispute the existence of infant immersion up to or even after 1584. His contention refers only to believers' immersion; but my argument is, that where we can trace believers' immersion back twenty-six years beyond where infant immersion is so prevalent, it compels the belief, other facts so strongly corroborating it, that believers' immersion must have been practiced during the same period, remembering, as we must, that under far more adverse circumstances, it had survived for fourteen centuries.

Before passing to other proofs of my position found in the book, let me call attention to another serious mistake I am certain the Doctor has made, and one that must have a most important bearing on the whole question at issue. I refer to his position in regard to Menno Simon, whom Baptists have always regarded as Baptist in principle and practice, but who Dr. Whitsitt tells us practiced sprinkling instead of immersion. The authority on which he asserts this is a so-called corrected translation of Menno's utterances on the subject, and is given on page 46.

A scholar named Morgan Edwards, it appears made a translation of Menno's statement, touching baptism as follows: "After we have searched ever so diligently, we shall find no other baptism besides dipping in water, which is acceptable to God, and maintained in His word." But now comes one Dr. Burrage and says the passage from Simon is not correctly translated, and gives the following as the correct one: "However diligently we seek, night and day, yet we find no more than one baptism in water, that is pleasing to God, expressed and contained in His word—namely, this baptism on faith." Forthwith, therefore, Brother Whitsitt gives up the translation of Edwards, adopts that of Burrage, and puts Menno Simon out of the Baptist fold.

But now, who is Dr. Burrage? And in what respect is he a more reliable witness than Edwards? Here is a translation that has stood for years as correct. Are we to give it up till we know something about the man who gives us the new? Is Dr. Burrage a disinterested witness? Is he a Baptist or a Pedobaptist? Is

he better able to give a correct translation
than Edwards? I must have information on
these points before I can consent to let go of
Menno Simon. I know of scores of professedly
learned men who contend that dipping or immersion is not the correct translation of the
Greek word "Baptiso." This we know to be
incorrect; is it not possible that this translation
of Dr. Burrage is also incorrect?

But now for argument's sake, I will admit the
Burrage translation to be the correct one.
What is the result? We have twice the testimony to the Baptistic principles and practices
of Menno Simon than we had before. The Edwards translation makes no reference to believers as being the only proper subjects of
Baptism. The Burrage translation proves
Menno to have been sound on this point, and
does not in the least weaken the testimony as
to the mode. Here are Burrage's own words:
"We shall find no more than one baptism in water, that is pleasing to God." The baptism of
Menno Simon was therefore that of a believer
only IN WATER. This makes him a Baptist.
You can't baptize a person IN WATER by putting
a few drops on his forehead. You can't baptize a person IN WATER by pouring a dipper full
over his head. If you can let us give up our
contention with the Pedobaptists and adopt
their mode of administration. But there is
only one way in which you can baptize a person IN WATER. That is by dipping him in the
water. This fact is as clear as the sunlight

and I must be excused if I refuse to follow the example of Brother Whitsitt, and surrender Menno Simon simply because Doctor Burrage says Morgan Edwards made a mistake in the translation. Menno Simon was undoubtedly a Baptist, so far as baptism goes, if the translation of Dr. Burrage is correct. Let us now test my position by the rule of logic.

A Baptist is one who baptises believers only, and who baptises only in water.

Menno Simon baptised believers only and baptised them only in water.

Therefore Menno Simon was a Baptist.

Menno Simon was a Baptist.
The Mennonites were followers of Menno Simon.

Therefore the Mennonites were Baptists.

The baptism of Smyth and his party was identical with that of the Mennonites (Whitsitt P. 59.)

The Baptism of the Mennonites was that of a believer in water, which is the baptism of the Baptists.

Therefore Smyth and his party were Baptists.

When Brother Whitsitt shall have proved this to be unsound logic, I will confess to having studied Bishop Whately in vain.

Granted, that some, even many of the Mennonites afterwards adopted the practice of sprinkling, which it is no doubt they did; they were no longer followers of Menno Simon and no longer entitled to the name of Mennonites.

"Menno's most definite expression," says Bro. Whitsitt, (P. 47,) "touching the act of baptism is found in the folio edition of his works, where he says, "I certainly think that these and similar commands, (to love one's enemies, etc.) are more painful and burdensome to perverted flesh, which is everywhere so prone to walk in its own way, than it is to receive a handful of water."

To this statement of our brother I have two answers. The first is, I think Brother Whitsitt again mistaken. This statement is not, in my judgment, "Menno's most definite expression." The most definite expression quoted by our brother is that which declares that "The only baptism that is acceptable to God and maintained in His word, is that of a believer in water." This is definite, clear cut, and leaves no doubt of his meaning.

My second answer is that this last statement has no bearing on his own practice, as to the mode of baptism. This statement is easily enough understood. He was there writing from the standpoint of his enemies. He was referring in a controversial way, to their practice, not his; and tells them that it is no doubt harder for them to follow the precepts of true Christianity than it was to receive their little handful of water baptism. This utterance, therefore, only strengthens, instead of weakens the position that Menno was a believer in, and practiced believers' baptism in water.

What then is the result of this fact proven beyond successful contradiction, that Menno Simon and his followers were Baptists and that Smyth and his party joined the Mennonites because their baptism was precisely alike? Brother Whitsitt has based his entire argument on the mistaken idea that Menno and his followers practiced sprinkling; this proven to be an error, and that they were Baptists, destroys his whole foundation and his superstructure falls. This fact I have proven beyond the shadow of a doubt from his own witnesses.

Now, what further proof does Dr. Whitsitt give us, in favor of reasonable probability, that immersion continued to be practiced in England? On page 21, he tells us that Professor Scheffer "claims that but very few Anabaptists practiced immersion." Even, therefore, Prof. Scheffer, himself a disbeliever in the practice, is compelled to admit that some did practice it. It would be interesting if Prof. Scheffer had told us just what proportion he regarded as very few. Others might differ from him there.

Page 35: "In fact, few Anabaptists anywhere were immersionists." Some of them, then, were. Page 37: "While the great body of Anabaptist believers practiced pouring and sprinkling, there were a few exceptions in favor of immersion." Was it not possible that a few of them were still in England, where, Dr.

Whitsitt tells us, immersion continued longer than anywhere else?

Page 38: "The people of St. Gall, whom Grebel baptised in the Sitter river on Palm Sunday, 1525, it is likely were immersed."

Page 39: "Clement Sender, an eye witness, describes the act of baptism in the river Lech; that it was immersion, except in times of persecution, when it was administered simply by sprinkling the forehead in cellars and barnyards!"

Same Page: "No sufficient reason appears for calling in question the authority of Sender. If it be allowed to stand, then we must conclude that the Anabaptists of Augsberg, at the most flourishing moment of their existence when their church numbered 1,100 members, practiced immersion as well as sprinkling."

Page 40: "There were immersing Anabaptists in Poland, Silesia, Luathania and Pomerania." Quite a respectable array of immersionists after all.

As a great majority of those immersions, at least, were outside of England, they furnish, of course, no positive proof that the same existed in England: but they do furnish strong circumstantial evidence. If there be so many exceptions to the rule elsewhere, it is reasonable to suppose there would be in England also. Add to this the facts that immersion prevailed in England long after it went out of general use elsewhere—that we can trace it forward by royal decrees to 1584, and then

back, as I have clearly shown to twenty-six
years beyond that point—that there is plain
reference to three kinds of Anabaptists in
England one of which the Doctor's own witness proves to have been immersionists, that
in spite of faggot and fire and imprisonment,
and every species of persecution and torture,
there had continued a people who had maintained their allegiance to Christ, through so
many long centuries—though "kept covered
under the ashes;" in England, they were yet
there, and I appeal to every unprejudiced reader, if I have not proven a reasonable probability, if it does not amount even to a certainty—
that immersion still survived in England during the period in which it is disputed. Remember, its existence is admitted, and a reasonable
probability of its continuance, is all I am required to establish.

What now is necessary on the Doctor's part,
to overthrow this position and maintain his
case? He must prove absolutely beyond any
reasonable doubt, by positive indisputable evidence, that there was not a single case of believers' immersion in England during the period
referred to; circumstantial evidence must be
ruled out, as insufficient to overthrow an established fact. The fact that a man can count
a thousand oak trees in a piece of woods is no
proof that the pine trees that stood there are not
there now. Similarly the fact that Brother
Whitsitt has shown that thousands of persons
practiced sprinkling and pouring in England,

during a certain period, is no proof that some-
body did not practice believers' immersion at
the same time. With such testimony, Brother
Whitsitt would fail to get a verdict in a case
involving one hundred dollars, before any
court in the United States. And yet this is
precisely the nature of his testimony, from beginning to end.

He relies largely on witnesses. Are those
witnesses competent to testify—not merely
that they can count a thousand oak trees, but
that the pine trees are not there. Permit me
to rely on his kind of testimony, and I will prove
that there is not a Baptist today in the United
States.

I am fully aware of the relative distinction
between "legal evidence" and "moral evidence,"—"Legal certainty" and "Moral certainty," and the argument that may be made there-
from; but this case comes under the domain of
the former, and nothing short of positive proof
can be accepted. We have a right to question
the witnesses. Do they know all the facts?
Have they gone into every nook and corner
where those persecuted people hid themselves, in the dark days when they were either
banished, or "kept covered under the ashes,"and
sought out every case of believers' baptism
that was administered? Have they made
themselves acquainted with the practice of
every preacher, and every church? Have they
visited every one of them in their midnight
conventicles, where they met to worship God in

secret, that they might manifest their allegiance
to Christ and his word, unseen by the keen eye
of their persecutors? This is what they must
have done to be competent witnesses in this
case.

I grant, for argument's sake, that Dr. Whitsitt has made a strong case—an incontroverti-
ble case—in all that he has attempted to do.
That, is to show that, during the period named,
there were thousands of Christians in England,
some of them called Anabaptists, who practiced sprinkling and pouring; but this is no
evidence that there may not have been others
who practiced something else. We can furnish the testimony of ten millions of people to
prove the custom of sprinkling in
this country, but that is no evidence
that there may not be a few Baptists
here who practice immersion. Yet that is precisely the nature of Brother Whitsitt's testimony. He furnishes, also, numerous cases of
individual pouring, to prove that nothing else
existed. Similarly, we can fill fifty books of
five hundred pages each, with reports of individual cases of sprinkling in this country, although we have three million Baptists as well.

Let it be remembered that during
those dark days for the Baptists in England,
that, in addition to the difficulty of keeping
proper records, it was dangerous for them to
do so. A few of their records have survived;
but will any man imagine that those few
records found in the British Museum and the

Bodlein Library, cover all the work done for Christ and his cause, during that period? Dr. Whitsitt makes the positive statement that believers' immersion had ceased to exist—"was a lost art"—in England, prior to 1641. He has only proven that a great many people, during that period, practiced something else.

The small amount of reliance to be put on the testimony furnished by the numerous quotations, to prove that "immersion was something new in 1641," and afterwards, will be readily understood, if we remember, first, that at that time the temporal sword had ceased to keep "the fire of their faith covered under the ashes," and argument and ridicule were the only weapons left with which to fight the Baptists, when they came out more openly with their practice; and second, that this has always been a favorable mode of warfare in the baptismal controversy. We all know how frequently we have heard the same epithets and insinuations of our recent origin, and the newness of our practice, even in our own day and in our own land, so that the argument from these is of very little value in the controversy.

There is neither desire nor necessity on my part to impeach any of Brother Whitsitt's witnesses, but it should not be overlooked, that those on whom he most strongly relies are adverse witnesses; and it is always a rule in evidence to take the testimony of an adverse witness with reasonable caution. While, therefore, their honesty is, no doubt, unquestionable, it is reasonable to suppose that their belief and practice, will more or less influence the conclusions which they form from their investigations. Still, giving due weight to every testimony brought forward, it is my firm conviction that Brother Whitsitt has not only failed to prove the claim he set up, but has furnished very strong presumptive evidence against himself.

Indeed I think there is needed no stronger evidence than that which Dr. Whitsitt himself furnishes to prove that believers' immersion did not require to be reintroduced in England in 1641.

I cannot close this brief sketch without expressing my high appreciation of the kind and gentle spirit, and Christ-like disposition our dear Brother Whitsitt has manifested through all this unfortunate controversy. He has shown us all an example of meekness, and Christian charity that we will do well to imitate. The fact that I think he is mistaken in the conclusion he has drawn from the testimony furnished, does not, in the least, shake my confidence in him as a sound Baptist, or my kind regard for him as a brother beloved. Calm as a rock he has stood, while the thunders of controversy have roared around him, and the storms of adverse criticism have beat upon him; and when this storm shall have all blown over, and the unpleasant things connected with it forgotten, the memory of that kind and gentle spirit will remain with us, like a benediction, and will anchor our brother more firmly than ever in the loving heart of our great denomination. Brother Whitsitt has kept his word, and given us all the reasons for the position he has taken. Let us each one study them, carefully, honestly, and form such conclusion in the matter, as our judgment shall dictate. Then let us all "shake hands across the bloody chasm," lay the matter aside, as one of the useful lessons we, as a denomination, have learned, and rally as one man to the great work our God has given us to do.